ALSO BY JENN BISHOP
The Distance to Home

14 Hollow Road

Jenn Bishop

ALFRED A. KNOPF

New York

Text copyright © 2017 by Jennifer Barnes
Jacket art copyright © 2017 by Erin McGuire

All rights reserved. Published in the United States by Alfred A. Knopf, an imprint of Random House Children's Books, a division of Penguin Random House LLC, New York.

Knopf, Borzoi Books, and the colophon are registered trademarks of Penguin Random House LLC.

Visit us on the Web! randomhousekids.com

Educators and librarians, for a variety of teaching tools, visit us at RHTeachersLibrarians.com

Library of Congress Cataloging-in-Publication Data is available upon request.
ISBN 978-1-101-93875-1 (trade) — ISBN 978-1-101-93876-8 (lib. bdg.)
ISBN 978-1-101-93877-5 (ebook)

The text of this book is set in 12.75-point Bembo.

Printed in the United States of America
June 2017
10 9 8 7 6 5 4 3 2 1

First Edition

To Elizabeth and Erin, for your many years of friendship.
(Thank goodness we never had crushes on the same boys!)

1

"Maddie, can you please hold still! For one more *murf-nurt.*"

Mom's mouth is full of bobby pins, but I know she meant "minute."

Standing on my toes is probably not the best way to hold still, but it's the best way for Mom to get at my hair.

She jabs another bobby pin deep into my skull. "Ow, Mom."

"Didn't mean to, honey. Almost done."

My best friend, Kiersten, who can do the yoga tree pose for ten minutes without falling over, says that the way to balance is to focus on one thing. If you can do that, you won't fall over. Like that's easy.

I try to find just one thing to stare at. It's actually

pretty hard since there are so many things covering my walls—posters, pictures of me and my friends, my bulletin board—and all of them jog my memory so that I turn my head a little and Mom tugs on my hair to hold me in place.

So instead, I look out the window. My neighbor Greta and her brother, Jeremy the Germ, are on their swing set. We call him the Germ because he gets every single stomach bug that goes around the school. I swear he must lick everyone; it's the only explanation. Jeremy's swinging so high I wonder if he'll flip over the top. I'm pretty sure Ms. Kaufman, the science teacher, would say he couldn't, but it sure looks like he could. That would make a cool science-fair project. Can a person swing hard and fast enough to go over the top of a swing set? I bet that'd get an A.

Greta is wearing a princess dress over her pajamas. I think she's yelling something at Jeremy, but I can't hear what because my window is closed.

Hank's bell jingles as he enters the room, and I turn my head the tiniest bit to see him. He bounds over with a slobbery tennis ball in his mouth. It falls to the floor with a bounce and rolls under my bed. I reach out my foot to try and grab it.

"Madelyn Hope!" Mom yanks my head so I'm facing the window again.

"Sorry," I whisper. "Are you done yet?" I try extra hard not to move my head while I ask the question.

Mom circles me, checking out my hair from all possible angles. Her face is squinty.

"Does it look okay?"

She reaches for the handheld mirror I keep on my bureau. "Take a look for yourself."

My hair, which normally falls down my back in messy curls, is attached to my head in huge interlocking braids. Mom grabs another handheld mirror from the bathroom so I can see the back. We're the only people I know who don't have any mirrors on the walls. Last week, Mom took them all down. She said something about how we live in a looks-based society and she's taking a stand. She'll probably put them back up when she realizes her new great idea means Dad has toothpaste in his beard when he heads off for work.

"It looks so cool," I say.

"You can learn anything on YouTube."

I hand the mirror back to her. All I can think about is what Kiersten said earlier this week. That she overheard someone saying that Avery wants to dance with me. What will he think of my hair?

Mom wipes some sweat off her forehead and redoes her bun. "Is it just me or is it way too hot for June?" She opens my window.

I reach under the bed and roll the tennis ball back to Hank. He's flopped out on the little spot of hardwood floor in my room that isn't covered by the rug. His chin rests on his paws, and his golden-brown ears are splayed out on the floor. The ball bumps his nose, but he doesn't even budge. He lifts his eyes up to me as if he's saying, *I can't move one more inch.* I don't blame him; I wouldn't want to be covered in fur on a day this hot either.

I open up my closet, where my dress has been hanging in plastic wrap ever since we got it at the mall three weeks ago. I try to step into it, but the fabric isn't stretchy enough. But if I have to put it on over my head, then . . .

"How am I going to get this on with my hair?"

"Don't worry, Mads." Mom reminds me about the hidden zipper on the side of the dress.

She snips off the two little strings that hooked the dress onto the hanger. I'm glad she knew to cut those off. I don't want to look like I have white strings shooting out of my armpits.

I do a twirl. "What do you think, Hank?" His ears perk up at the sound of his name.

"Hot dog," Mom says in her Hank voice.

I sit on the living room couch, eating Goldfish graham crackers because Mom's afraid if I eat anything colored or sticky or liquid, I'll stain my dress.

"How come Maddie gets to go to the dance and I can't?" Cameron's sitting on the cushion next to me, but he wants Mom to hear all the way in the kitchen, so he whines extra loud.

I turn up the volume on the TV.

"Maddie, that's too loud." Mom pops her head into the living room. "Cammie, this dance is a special treat for the sixth graders before they go on to junior high. This is the last time it'll be just Maddie and all the kids from our town. Next year, there will be four other towns of kids going to school with your sister."

"How long till I'm in sixth grade, again?"

"I thought Mrs. Kenary taught subtraction this year," I say.

Cam shakes his head, still waiting for his answer.

"Five, Cammie. *Five*. I felt the same way you do every year until now. You'll get your turn."

Cam sighs and refocuses on his TV show.

Dad comes in through the front door with two huge pizza boxes. Cam runs to meet him. "Daddy! Maddie's all dressed up!"

Dad undoes the top button of his shirt. "I thought I was going to roast on the car ride home." He rests the pizzas on the entry table and takes off his suit jacket. "Hey, Cam. Hey, Mads! Can you put on the weather? They said something about thunderstorms. Wouldn't that be a godsend. I swear, the garden's not going to make it with the water ban and—"

"Dad!" He stops as I stand up and twirl around in

my dress so he can see my hair and the dangly earrings I borrowed from Mom.

"Don't you look fancy-pants? You sure you're not the latest contestant on *Dancing with the Stars*? You psyched for the dance?"

I nod like crazy. I've only been picturing it in my head all week. It's a good thing there aren't any tests in the very last week of school. The teachers must know everybody would flunk them.

"Did you feed Hank yet?"

I shake my head. "Mom let him out."

"Even fancy-pants almost-seventh-graders have to do their chores." Dad gives me that look.

I head out into the backyard. The air is thick and muggy, like the upstairs bathroom when we all take showers in a row. "Hank! Suppertime!" I listen for the jingle of his collar bell. After checking his usual spots—his under-the-porch sleeping hideout and his favorite tree—I walk over to Greta and Jeremy's swing set.

Greta flies off the swing, landing firmly on her feet. "You look pretty, Maddie."

"Pretty stinky," the Germ says. He pokes his head out of the wooden tower attached to the swing set.

"If you see Hank, can you drag him over? I've got to leave for the dance and it's time for his dinner."

"Maybe he's someone else's dinner." Jeremy snorts. "We learned about the food chain in science today."

"Gross." I want to say that no animal would stand a chance against Hank, but we all know that's not true. He may be the biggest dog in the neighborhood, but he's also the wimpiest.

"Maddie! Time to go!" Dad calls out to me from the front yard. He's changed into shorts and a T-shirt. "Don't want to keep the fellas waiting."

"Nobody calls them 'fellas,' Dad." I roll my eyes. "It's not that kind of dance, anyway."

Dad hands me my dress shoes, the ones I had to beg and beg Mom to buy for me. She says I'll have to do extra chores for the whole summer to pay her back, but oh, it's worth it. They shimmer when I move my feet and they've got two-inch heels. I slide my feet into them and take a few wobbly steps.

"Almost as tall as me," Dad says. Even with these shoes on, I barely reach Dad's shoulder. "Come on, kiddo."

Dad backs the car onto the road and changes the radio station to the Red Sox game. After a few minutes, a loud beep interrupts the game. A man's voice comes on and says there's a severe thunderstorm warning and lists all the counties.

"Yeah, yeah, yeah. Get back to the game," Dad says.

I reach my hand around the back of my head and touch my hair. It's perfect, if a little sticky. Even the breeze can't mess with it. Mom used what seemed like an entire container of hair spray to make sure of that.

I roll down the window and rest my arm on the ledge.

At the end of the inning, the radio switches to a commercial. Dad lowers the volume. "You found Hank and gave him his supper, right?"

"He didn't come when I called."

"Mads, why didn't you say anything?"

I stare down at my sparkly shoes. "Sorry." I just can't think about anything besides Avery and what it's going to be like to dance with him.

"Guess you'll be doing Cammie's chores tomorrow to make up for it."

"Fine," I say.

Who cares about tomorrow? All I can think about is tonight and how we waited the whole year for this. Me and Kiersten and the entire sixth grade are going to have the best night ever. No—not *the best night ever.* That's so fifth grade. *Epic.* That's what Kiersten's older brother, Bryant, would say. Tonight is going to be epic.

When I step into the school gym, I can't believe we ever played volleyball and badminton in here. The overhead lights are off, but Christmas lights are strung across the walls, and there's a disco ball turning above the center of the room, making the floor sparkle. Red and white streamers—Hitchcock Elementary's colors—stretch from the bleachers up to the ceiling. How did they even get them up there?

"Maddie!"

Over by the snacks, Kiersten is waving at me. She's standing with the new girl, Gabriella, but she looks so dressed up, so different from how she looks in school, that I have to do a double take. My shoes won't let me run, so instead I walk over, very ladylike.

"I love your dress," I say. Kiersten is wearing a sparkly

green dress that stops at her knees, and her long blond hair is up in a bun. It looks like her mom let her wear makeup. Thick mascara, blush, and lipstick. I rub my lips together. All I have on is ChapStick.

Gabriella's wearing a short black skirt, a tank top, a jean jacket, a really cool jade-and-orange necklace. Didn't she know we were getting dressed up for this dance? That it's something special? I feel almost bad for her, but she doesn't seem freaked out about us all being fancier than her.

"Your hair looks pretty," Gabriella says.

I touch it to make sure it's all still up. "Can you believe my mom did this?"

Kiersten shakes her head. "I'm surprised she let you get dressed up. Didn't she say you weren't supposed to care about how you look?"

I shrug.

"Well, at least she didn't try to have a *talk* with you about the dance," Kiersten says.

"What kind of talk?" Gabriella asks, munching on a potato chip.

"My mom said that I need to stay an arm's length away from whoever I dance with." Kiersten reaches out her arm to demonstrate. "A whole arm? *Come on, Mom.* You get closer than that dancing in a group."

"I'm definitely planning to get a lot closer than an arm." Gabriella nods.

A hand, then? I still don't know Gabriella that well

and I don't want to sound dumb by asking. I wonder who she wants to dance with. Maybe Kiersten knows.

"Me too," Kiersten says. "Anyway, it's not like my mom sent someone here to spy on me. She'll never know."

I nibble on a cookie while Kiersten tells us all about this tiny vintage shop in Northampton where her mom helped her find her dress.

The wall behind the snack table is lined with photos from every year we've been at the elementary school. There's one of me and Kiersten from kindergarten. She's missing her two front teeth, and I'm rocking some seriously curly pigtails and an Elmo shirt. And another of me and Kiersten in the third-grade holiday concert in our matching red sequined sweaters. Man, were we dorky.

One picture looks like it was tacked on at the last minute. Like they realized they didn't have any picture of Gabby and didn't want her to feel left out. Gabriella, Kiersten, and the other kids from Kiersten's street waiting for the bus together. Probably taken a week ago.

I spot a picture of me and Avery as cows in the school play in third grade. Gregg kept trying to milk him, and Avery told Mrs. Whitman that a guy cow isn't supposed to have udders, and then Mrs. Whitman got flustered and said all cows have udders, even bulls. Turns out she was wrong. Avery's always been so smart, even in third grade. He's been the smartest one in our grade for as long as I can remember.

It's hard to believe that Avery and I were in day care together at the house of that one lady whose name I can't remember who had bedsheets covering her sofas. Or that two years ago, Kiersten and I would play around in the woods behind Avery's house, trying to spy on him and Gregg in their fort. He was just Avery then. Just my neighbor Avery. And now he isn't.

Now he's the one whose head I stare at the back of during social studies when I'm supposed to be writing my essay about Roanoke Colony, but instead I'm imagining what it would be like to kiss him. The one who I try to sit near—but not next to—on the bus every day. The one who I write about a little—okay, *a lot*—in my diary.

I keep looking toward the door, waiting for Avery to walk through, watching as kids from my class slowly fill up the room. There are seventy kids in my grade, which always felt like a ton, but in the fall, there will be five times as many. That many people wouldn't even fit in this gym.

Finally, I see him. He's dressed up in a pale blue shirt and khakis. No tie, though. Some of the other boys have on ties. He comes in with Gregg and Naveen, and they head straight toward the snack table, toward us.

All of a sudden I'm not ready for him to see me. What if he thinks my hair is crazy? Maybe Kiersten and Gabriella were only pretending they like it. And what if my breath stinks? I try to breathe it in, but all I can smell is chocolate chip cookie. I chuck the rest of my cookie behind the table, hoping no one sees, and grab Kiersten and Gabriella. There's no way the boys are coming out on the dance floor right away. That'll buy me some time. "You ready to dance?" I pull them toward the center of the gym.

The DJ—the librarian's husband, who also works at the post office—switches to a faster song. I'm glad I didn't go with the first dress I tried on. Mom was right—it really would have been too tight to dance in. I raise my hands in the air and bob my head, shifting my feet from side to side. It's not so different from dancing around Kiersten's basement with the music turned way up.

The dance floor is filled with mostly girls until Gregg pushes his way through. Some of the guys follow him, though they don't really look like they want to be dancing. Gregg starts jumping up and down, flailing his arms in the air. Classic Gregg.

I peek over at Avery. He's moving a little bit, but I wouldn't call what he's doing dancing. It's hard to keep track of him with everyone dancing and laughing and the lights so dim.

When the music switches to a hip-hop song, the crowd forms a circle and people take turns dancing in the center. I try to stay behind someone so I don't get pushed in. Dancing at Kiersten's house is one thing, but I'm not ready to put on a show for the entire sixth grade.

The girls in gymnastics and dance are the first ones to take turns. They dance and bend in ways I'm pretty sure my body can't. Gregg sneaks in and flops around on the floor like a worm. He has his tie wrapped around his head like he's a ninja, even though we've only been here for twenty minutes.

"Gregg's ridiculous," Gabriella says, laughing.

Yeah, Gregg's something special, all right.

Gregg freestyles in the center for a minute and then yells for Mr. C. to come into the circle.

Mr. C. is popping and locking, but it isn't until he gets down on the floor that we pretty much flip.

"I didn't know Mr. C. could do the windmill," Kiersten shouts over the music.

"Me neither! He's good."

We all chant, "Mr. C., Mr. C., Mr. C.!" And the next thing I know, Kiersten isn't standing next to me anymore. Avery is.

"Guess this is what he does when he's not grading math tests," Avery says.

"Probably practicing in his basement."

Avery smiles. His short brown hair looks a little bit slick, like he put gel in it for the dance. But there's still those freckles on his nose, and his eyes are that sharp, crisp blue like that shirt Mom makes Dad wear when they go on dates—the one she calls his handsome shirt.

I've sat next to Avery about a million times since kindergarten, in school or on the bus, but standing next to him, both of us dressed up like we're trying to be someone else, someone more grown-up—it's different. I don't know what to say. The million random ideas and thoughts that float around my head all day have flown away.

"How'd you do on the math final?" he asks.

"One-oh-four. How about you?"

"One-oh-two. How'd you get the second bonus question? It was impossible. I looked in the book after, and I still couldn't figure it out."

"It's all in here." I tap the side of my head.

The DJ changes to a slow song by Taylor Swift and I can feel it. *This is it.*

My mouth goes all cottony and I look at Avery, who's staring right back at me. Everything happens in slow motion. He opens his mouth. He doesn't even have to ask; I'll say yes.

But then he turns around.

And asks Gabriella.

3

Kiersten catches me as I stand alone, practically frozen in place watching Avery and Gabriella. She mouths, "What happened?"

I can't open my mouth and tell her because I don't know. Avery doesn't want to dance with me. He wants to dance with Gabriella. He *is* dancing with Gabriella. And I need to find someone else to dance with so I can stop thinking about Avery, because if I think about him for one more second, I know I'm going to cry.

I lock eyes with Gregg, whose tie is no longer wrapped around his head. "You want to dance?"

Gregg's one of the few guys in our class who are even shorter than me, but I don't care. All I know is, I can't let Avery see me standing alone right now. I rest my hands on Gregg's shoulders and he places his hands around my waist. He kind of smells, like maybe he didn't put on enough deodorant for this much dancing. He holds me closer than I want him to, but I don't ask him to back off. He probably thinks I really want to dance with him.

Wait. What if he thinks I actually want to dance *with him*? I try to pull away the tiniest bit, but instead he holds on to me even tighter.

We slowly turn and I see Kiersten resting her head on Naveen's shoulder. She smiles when she sees me. I bite my lip. My first slow dance is *not* supposed to be like this. It's not supposed to be with *Gregg,* who's gotten kicked out of Mr. C.'s class for spontaneously turning into a chicken more times than I can count.

I sing along in my head with Taylor Swift. I've probably listened to this song a thousand times before, but now it feels like I'm hearing it for the first time. She understands how stupid boys are.

When the song finally ends, I pull away from Gregg. He stares back at me with this goofy smile on his face, and something tells me he's going to ask me to dance during the next slow song unless I do something about it first.

Whatever the opposite of *epic* is, this is it.

Gabriella and Avery pull apart, but I don't watch like I'm right here and anyone can see me. I watch like it's a movie.

It's supposed to be me. *I* was supposed to star in that movie.

"Let's go to the bathroom." Kiersten tugs at my hand and I follow her across the gym, through all of my classmates who are still having a good time.

The bathroom is the one place the decorating committee forgot. Inside are the same barf-green stalls and grimy tile that have always been here. Bits of streamers that got stuck to people's feet litter the floor. There's no room in front of the mirror as girls redo each other's hair or put on another layer of lip gloss. We all looked shiny and perfect on the dance floor, but under the fluorescent lights, you can see who's wearing gobs of makeup to cover zits and who still hasn't started shaving her legs.

"It's just one song," Kiersten says.

"Yeah. One slow song. And he asked Gabriella. Gabriella! Not me." I chew on the inside of my lip.

"Maybe she just didn't know what else to do," Kiersten says.

"You wouldn't have said yes."

I'm watching Kiersten's face as she thinks it through. She waits one second too long to reply. And then everything goes black.

In the darkness, I let out a little yelp and reach my hand out to grab Kiersten's. "I can't see!" someone screams from inside one of the stalls. It sounds like Hailey Anderson.

Kiersten grips my hand tightly. She's always been afraid of the dark.

But not me. I wait for my eyes to adjust. "The power went out," I say. "That's it."

I wonder if Gabriella is still out there with Avery. If she's holding his hand in the dark.

The red exit sign casts a glow over the bathroom and slowly my eyes adjust, until I can make out the sink and the girls standing against it. It's like someone froze us in place when the lights went out.

Ms. Harrington, my old homeroom teacher, opens the bathroom door and shines a flashlight on us. "The generator's not kicking in like it's supposed to," she says. "Go out into the gym. I'll help you see to wash your hands and finish up in here if you need to."

Someone whispers, "I can't see the toilet paper."

Kiersten and I head back into the gym. Kids are sitting on the floor or standing around in clumps. No one has a clue what's going on. Does the blackout mean the dance is canceled now?

"Stay put, folks." Mr. C.'s booming voice carries through the din. "We're hoping to get the generator up and running."

"Was there a storm or something?" Kiersten asks.

I remember the warning that cut into the Red Sox game on the radio. "The music was so loud. Guess we missed it."

With no music and no dancing, everyone is crowding

around the food. I spy Avery over by the chips, but then I see that he's still with Gabriella. "I want to get my phone," I say, and we head over to where we left our bags.

When I take out my phone, I see a long list of missed calls from Mom's cell phone.

I text Mom that we lost power at the dance, that we're not sure if it's over or not.

I'm not the only one trying to touch base with someone back home. Soon nearly everyone has their cell phones pressed to their ears, trying to reach their parents. Meanwhile, Mr. C. keeps telling us not to go anywhere. He says something about the whole town being without power.

"I bet we're the only class that has ever lost power in the middle of the sixth-grade dance," Kiersten says, picking at her nail polish.

Someone's cell phone rings next to us in the bleachers. It's not one of those generic ringtones, but the song they play in the eighth inning at Fenway Park. Avery's phone.

He runs over toward us and I try not to look at him.

"What? Mom? I can't—you're not coming through clear," he says.

Kiersten is watching him, too. I think about how she hesitated when I asked what she would do if Avery asked her to dance. Does she have a crush on Avery?

Avery's butt hits the bleachers hard as he sits down.

He startles me, so it's okay to look. At least, that's what I tell myself. There's something in his voice that's changed.

His hand, the one holding the phone, is shaking.

"Okay, okay. I'm not going anywhere. I'm right here. I'm safe."

He places the phone on the metal bleacher with a bang.

He turns toward me. "Maddie?" His voice is just as shaky as his hand. What happened to the confident Avery from math class, the one who always knows the answers to all of Mr. C.'s questions?

"Yeah?"

"Call home."

Before I get a chance to call home, Mr. C. uses his someone's-in-trouble voice. It cuts through all the chatter in the room. A few people are still whispering until he yells, "Hey!" and then everybody gets real quiet.

"I'm sorry to be the one to have to tell you this, but we have no choice but to cancel the dance."

Across the room, some of the kids start talking again, but I'm still stuck on what Avery just said—*Call home*—and the fact that I still haven't.

Mr. C. shushes everyone. "The power substation is shot. We're not going to be getting power back anytime soon, folks. I . . ." Suddenly Mr. C. sounds like he has something caught in his throat. "I don't know how to tell you this. Can't believe it myself, really. These kinds of things don't happen here." He clears his throat.

"The thunderstorms spawned a tornado that crossed the western side of town."

I hear someone gasp. *Western side.* Which side of town is the western side? All the missed calls from Mom. Is my house—are we on the western side of town?

Mrs. Gleason from the library steps up next to Mr. C. "We're putting out a robocall to your parents letting them know the dance is canceled, but I have a feeling a lot of them are already on their way."

I call Mom's cell number and press the phone to my ear. *Pick up. Pick up. Please, pick up.*

It goes straight to voice mail. "Mom, it's Maddie. They told us about the tornado. Please, call me back."

I stare at the phone in my hand, willing it to ring, and chew on the inside of my cheek. Probably everyone's trying to reach someone on a cell phone. That's why I can't get through. It has to be.

"My mom said we can give you a ride." Avery's voice isn't shaky anymore, but it's not his normal voice either.

"Did she talk to my mom?"

Avery shakes his head. "She just said she'd be here soon. And something about it being a close call." He slides his phone back into his pocket. "Want to go outside and wait?"

I scan the crowd for Kiersten, but everyone is frantic, and I can't find her.

Outside are at least a dozen other kids, plus a long line of cars in the pickup circle. Kayla Cassidy's mom yells out her name and Kayla runs toward her. Her mom kisses her on her forehead, even though there's a ton of people who can see.

I stare down at my phone.

Come on, Mom. Call me back.

There are sirens in the distance, but right in front of the school, it's way quiet. The concrete steps are scratchy against my bare legs. I kick off my shoes. There's no reason to be dressed up anymore.

I keep thinking about the thing I always told myself when I was little and the thunder got so loud it shook my house. I'd camp out on the rug next to my parents' bed. Cammie was just a baby then, so it was all four of us in the room. No, five. Hank was always there, too. Hank hates storms.

Tornadoes don't like hills, I'd tell myself. Tornadoes happen out west, where it's flat for miles and miles and miles. They don't happen in New England. Not in Hitchcock, Massachusetts. And especially not on Hollow Road, where everyone's house is surrounded by forest.

Avery sits down next to me. He's jiggling his leg, like he always does right before a test. Did he get taller? His pants are a little too short again.

"I'm sure they'll call soon," he says. "The cell towers get overloaded anytime there's a disaster."

I swallow hard. "Right."

With each passing minute, there are fewer and fewer of us waiting outside the school. Finally, a red minivan pulls up in front of us and Avery leaps up from the stairs. The passenger-side window rolls down. I know that face.

"Dad!" I run toward him, my shoes in my hand.

Dad opens the door when he sees me. I barrel into him and he hugs me close. Sequins must be falling off my dress but I don't care.

When we finally pull apart, I notice a cut on his forehead. His face—it's dirty.

"Sorry I wasn't here sooner, hon. I couldn't find my car," he says.

"What happened to it?" I ask.

Dad furrows his eyebrows as he stares back at me. He doesn't answer my question.

"Where's Mom? And Cammie? They're okay, right?"

Dad nods. "They're okay, honey. We're all okay."

I climb into the backseat next to Avery and we head toward our street.

"How's the house?" I ask.

"Our street was hit pretty bad."

I try to listen as Dad tells us about what happened. How the sky was this weird green color he'd never seen before. How the wind died down and it got still. So still. He and Mom went down in the basement with

Cammie, just in case. And Cammie really had to pee, so they made him pee in a bucket in the basement. They weren't taking any chances.

I stare out the window at the houses as we pass them by. Tidy yards. Cars parked in front of garages. Swing sets. It doesn't seem possible that a big, whirling, destructive mass blew through the other side of town. But when I see Dad's dirty, scratched face in the rearview mirror, I know it must have.

"What about the Germ and Greta?"

"The Manoukians are okay, too."

Dad turns to look at Mrs. Linden, Avery's mom, and there's this look on her face. The weird thing is, Dad has that look, too. Dad hardly ever gets frazzled. The only thing that can get Dad worked up is the Red Sox or the Patriots.

Avery's mom doesn't put on the blinker to make the turn for our street. "Where are we going?" I ask.

"You can't go that way. Too many trees are down. That's why it took us so long to get to the school," she says.

Rolling down the window, I hear a siren. Soon it's not the only one.

As the sirens grow louder, I dig my nails—the nails Mom and I painted glittery blue just last night for the dance—into the palms of my hands. Red and blue lights flash up ahead. I can see more in the rearview mirror.

Avery's mom pulls the car over to the side of the road

to let an ambulance pass. A fire truck barrels by next, and behind it are three—no, four—police cars.

I glance over at Avery. He has his thumb up to his mouth. He's chewing at the skin around his thumbnail. Nobody is talking anymore. Not even Dad and Avery's mom.

I crawl my hand out to the center of the seat between the two of us. The ambulance, fire truck, and police cars are all at the turn up ahead. They're heading for Hollow Road. That's when it clicks. This isn't some story on the news that I'm watching with Mom, something that happened hundreds of miles away to perfect strangers. The scratches on Dad's head. The fact that I'm in Avery's mom's car, not Dad's. This is real life. My life.

Avery folds his hand around mine and gives me a squeeze. My heart does that jumpy thing it does in class sometimes when I'm looking at Avery and he's busy taking notes. Kiersten says it's creepy and I need to stop doing it—the looking—but she does the same thing with Naveen all the time. And anyway, I can't stop. It's not that easy.

But this isn't like all the other times. Avery's hand is cold and clammy and he's not even smiling. There's no way he's going to kiss me, like I thought could maybe happen tonight, if for once my life were like a movie.

I squeeze back.

"You're holding your breath," Avery says.

I let it out, staring at all the red lights in front of us. The traffic is bumper to bumper.

Even though it's taking forever to get home, Avery doesn't let go.

My hand is so sweaty I think about wiping it on the seat, but I don't. I need something to hold on to that feels real, because right now everything feels like a dream. A nightmare, really. Everything except Avery's hand on mine.

By the time we make the turn up our street, the sky is darker than normal for a little after eight-thirty. It's more than just the clouds. Suddenly I realize what's so different. None of the streetlights are working. And with the power out, there are no lights on in any of the houses.

Mrs. Linden said lots of trees were down, but so far everything looks just fine.

Avery is the first one to say anything. "Holy—"

"Avery, please," his mom says.

In one yard, it looks like someone cut off the tops of the trees with a scissors. In the next, the trees are chopped lower, split in half, or worse—lying on their sides, roots up in the air. One house is missing a roof. Another is half a house. Everything from inside is strewn all over the lawn: broken windows, the pink cotton-candy-looking fluff that goes inside walls, piles of bricks. There's a tree folded over a car, too, but then the next house is kind of okay.

It doesn't make sense.

Mr. Chen from down the street is using his chain saw to free a car in his driveway from a tree that's toppled over.

I feel like a little kid, pressing my face against the window as we pass by Avery's house. Wanting to see how bad it is and not wanting to see at the same time.

The big tree at the edge of his front yard, the one with the tire swing, is split down the middle. I don't see the tire swing anywhere.

Avery's voice cracks as he pulls his hand away from mine. "Mom, you said it wasn't that bad."

Their roof is gone. The whole upstairs is opened up like a dollhouse. The lawn is covered with stuff: a toilet on its side, broken windows and shutters, and more of that pink fluff.

Seeing that cotton-candyish stuff all over Avery's yard gives my stomach a sick feeling. Cotton candy is supposed to be a good thing, a fun treat. But there's too much of it. And it's not supposed to be on the outside. The outside and the inside are all mixed up. If that's what Avery's house looks like and it's *not that bad,* what does mine look like?

"It's fixable," Mrs. Linden says.

I dig my fingernails into the palms of my hands again as the car climbs further up the hill. We're getting closer to where the center of the tornado came through. I wish I knew the name for it. Maybe kids in the Midwest know about tornadoes, but we barely learn about them in science class. All I know is, each yard we pass is a little bit worse than the one before it.

I always thought a tornado came through and spun things around and then left it all behind. A big jumbled mess. But it's like it took stuff with it. There's less there.

Avery's mom pulls into Greta and the Germ's driveway. I know it's their driveway because that's their mailbox at the end, MANOUKIAN, and that's their house, still standing, but their yard isn't even recognizable. All of the trees at the edge of their yard and ours have been flattened, if they're there at all.

"Thanks for the ride, Naomi," Dad says.

"You need a place to stay tonight?" Mrs. Linden asks. "We're going over to the Simpsons' house."

"We'll be all set for the night."

I fumble with my seat belt.

"Maddie," Avery says.

My hand trembles as I open the door and step out into the still, humid air. I hold my shoes in my hand, my feet bare.

"It's gone, isn't it?" I ask Dad.

"Mom and Cammie are inside, honey. There's nothing we can do now that it's getting dark."

I start walking toward our yard, or where I think it is. My house is—was—set back from the street, so you could barely see it peeking out from behind the trees. But with so many of the trees that were here just hours ago now missing, it's hard to tell where I am. "I need to see it."

"Maddie!" Dad yells. "Your feet. There's broken glass everywhere."

I slip into my shoes and keep walking, stepping around bits of torn-off branches, shingles that belong to some house down the street. I wobble and almost fall over at one point, but I right myself just in time.

And then I'm standing in front of my house. Where it used to be. Now it's just some beams sticking up into the sky. A pile of wood and bricks. Our house wasn't even brick.

The space where my bedroom should be, tucked into the corner upstairs, is just a pocket of air. It's as dark as midnight. Up ahead, the clouds part, revealing a sky dotted with stars.

My home is gone.

A piece of glass in the yard reflects the moon above. No—not a piece of glass. My handheld mirror.

6

"You were inside the house—you were in there when . . ." My voice trembles. They crawled out of that mess. Mom and Dad and Cammie, they were trapped under all of that. When Mom was calling me, again and again, were they under there?

Dad rests his hand on my shoulder. "We're all safe, Maddie. That's the only thing that matters."

I hear a dog barking from up the street. "Is Hank at the Manoukians', too?"

"Maddie." Now it's Dad's voice that does the breaking.

I clench my hand into a fist. "Where's Hank?"

"He never came when we called him for supper, honey."

I start toward the debris. "We need to look for him."

I turn on my phone's flashlight, but it's not enough. "Dad, do you have a flashlight?"

I grab at pieces of wood with my bare hands, pushing some aside. I can barely see what's in front of me, never mind what's under all the rubble. "Hank?"

Dad pulls me back. "He wasn't in the house during the storm. He's not in here, Mads. We already did a sweep when it was still light out."

"Hank!" I yell. He can hear me, right? He always comes when I call. Almost always. "Hank!" I try my best to whistle, but chain saws are still buzzing down the hill and there's no way he can hear me unless he's close by. "Hank!" I shout even louder. "Hank, I'm here! Hank, come on. Hank!"

"We need to get inside," Dad says, "or somebody's going to get hurt out here."

"But Hank could be hurt. He's all alone." In my head, I picture Hank's tail sticking out from under a fallen tree. "What if he's trapped?"

Dad rubs my back. "It's not going to help to get hysterical about it. For all we know, Hank is in a neighbor's house up the street. There's broken glass and power lines down everywhere, hon. It's not safe to be out here. We can look more in the morning."

I suck in a deep breath, remembering what Avery said in the car.

"Maddie!"

This time it's Mom calling out my name. She's at the

edge of the Manoukians' yard. I run as fast as my fancy shoes will let me until she's wrapping her arms around me, lifting me onto my tippy-toes, hugging me close to her chest.

"Oh, Maddie." She doesn't try to be careful with my hair. It's all smooshed and messed up now. "We tried calling and calling you."

"Me too. It kept going to voice mail."

"We found each other and we're safe. That's all that matters."

"But Hank," I say.

Mom squeezes my shoulder. "I'm sure we'll find him in the morning."

Together with Dad, we walk back toward the Manoukians' house. Inside, their mantel is lit up with candles. Every flashlight and camping lantern in the house has been put to use, scattered around the floor or in somebody's hand, lighting the room.

"That's only three," Cammie says. He's playing Connect Four with Greta and the Germ on the living room floor.

He leaps up when he sees me. "Maddie!" He hugs my legs extra tight. "You missed it, you missed the tornado. It was so scary, Mads. Mommy and Daddy wouldn't let me go upstairs to go to the bathroom and I had to pee in a bucket. We hid in the basement. And the tornado"—he rolls his hands one over the other—"went right over our house. It was *so* scary."

"It sounds scary."

"So scary," he says again. And this time I see it in his fingers, the way he taps and taps them against his legs. I want to grab his hand, tell him to stop tapping, but I stop myself.

Maybe I'd be tapping, too, if I'd been here when it happened.

I sit down on the floor with him and the other kids.

"We hid in our basement, too." Greta twists a strand of hair between her fingers, her eyes still extra wide, like the shock of everything that happened hasn't worn off for her either.

In the kitchen, Mom and Dad are both talking on their cell phones. I wonder where we're going to sleep tonight.

Mrs. Manoukian comes into the living room. "Do you want something to eat, Maddie? I've got a whole fridge and freezer's worth of food that's about to spoil if we don't get the power back tonight. Ice cream? Glass of milk? Yogurt? You're not lactose intolerant, right?"

Cammie's head pops up. "Ice cream?"

"I think you've already had enough for tonight, kiddo."

"Maybe just a glass of milk." I follow Mrs. Manoukian into the kitchen.

"On hold again? I've been on hold for over an hour!" Mom sighs as she puts her phone on speaker, allowing staticky elevator music to fill the quiet. "Unbelievable." She runs her fingers through her hair.

"Who are you calling?" I ask.

"Just the—"

"Nothing you need to worry about." Dad mouths something to Mom.

Mrs. Manoukian hands me a glass of milk. "Sure you don't want anything else? I've got some leftover tuna salad."

I take a sip from the glass. "I'm fine."

Back in the living room, Greta, the Germ, and Cammie keep playing Connect Four like nothing even happened. Like we lost power because of a snowstorm and all we have to do is wait patiently for the electric company to get it back on. Like the snow will melt and everything will return to normal. It's so dark outside you can't see anything, but I can't pretend it'll look better in the morning.

Greta leans against the side of the couch with her eyes closed and her mouth hanging wide open. She's probably exhausted from all the excitement.

Cammie sticks another black piece through the slot. It clinks when it hits the bottom. "One, two, three, four. I win!" He looks up at me. "Maddie, I won!"

"You did," I say. "Good job."

He's smiling so wide. He can't tell that Jeremy let him win, scattering reds all over the board on purpose.

Cammie's only six, and when you're six, winning is everything.

"You want to play, Maddie?"

"Sure." I stretch my legs out on the floor, since that's the only way to sit in a dress this short.

"Black or red?"

"I don't care. Whichever color you don't want."

The music coming from Mom's cell phone stops playing in the other room. I try to listen to what she's saying.

"Maddie, it's your turn!"

I plink a black piece through the slot.

"I wanted to put mine there," Cammie says.

"Sorry."

"It's okay. Everyone makes mistakes."

He thinks extra hard about where to put his red piece and chews on his bottom lip. This one time, Dad and I were playing Connect Four when Hank was still a puppy. It was my job to pick up all the pieces and put the game away, but somehow I left out a piece and Hank ate it. We didn't know until later that day when he started acting all funny. It turns out you can't digest Connect Four pieces.

It was a red piece, the one he ate.

I run my fingers over the ridges of the black piece in my hand.

My mistakes. It was my turn to feed Hank tonight and I didn't. The only thing on my mind was Avery and the dance, not feeding Hank his supper. I should have kept looking for him.

"Maddie. Come on, it's your turn."

I put my piece in.

"Three in a row. Oh no! Oh no, oh no."

I glance at the board. Cammie's right. Without trying, I have three black pieces all in a row, with open slots on either side, and he only gets one turn before my next one. No matter what he does, I'm going to win.

He slides his red piece in with a quiet sigh, and I pop in my final black piece.

Cammie counts them out. "One, two, three, four. Maddie wins!"

I reach over to slide the bottom of the board and let the pieces all come crashing out.

7

I wake up in darkness, roll onto my stomach, and listen to the breathing. Slow, even breaths with a bit of snore. Dad. That's when I remember where I am: on the floor of the Manoukians' living room. Cammie is asleep upstairs in the trundle bed in the Germ's room. Down here it's just me and Mom and Dad.

A red light glows from the corner across the room. The power must have come back on while we were sleeping. The fridge hums in the kitchen. The light must be from their DVR.

Now everything that was on our DVR—all the shows I was going to catch up on this weekend—is gone.

I flip onto my other side so I can't see that little red light anymore. But when I close my eyes, it's still there. I can see it inside my head, taunting me.

How could a tornado hit one house but then leave the one next door untouched?

Why did it have to hit ours?

I hear Mom roll over, and I wonder if she's awake, too. Slowly the red light behind my eyelids fades away, until it's just me and the darkness and Dad's little snores.

I wake up to the buzzing chain saws, the hiss of the Manoukians' espresso machine, and helicopters. There are no shades in the living room, and the bright sunshine is as harsh as the noise outside.

Mom and Dad are already up and dressed and in the kitchen. Mrs. Manoukian's clothes are so baggy on Mom, but Mr. Manoukian and Dad are about the same size.

"You ready to help?" Dad asks me as he finishes off his piece of toast. "It's going to be an all-hands-on-deck kind of morning."

"Do you have your phone charger? I need to charge mine and then I can start calling around about Hank." I pour some milk in my bowl of Cocoa Krispies.

Dad points to a phone charger on the wall. "Mads, we're going to need your help today. We need everyone busting their butts outside with cleanup. There's a lot of work to do. Folks are still assessing the damage."

"But—"

"I want to find Hank every bit as much as you do,

41

honey. It's early still. I'm hopeful we'll hear something by the end of the day." Dad takes a sip of his coffee. "Hank's got his tag on, so whoever finds him will know to call us."

The *chop-chop-chop* of the helicopters overhead makes it hard for me to think.

"What's up with the helicopters?"

"News coverage," Dad says. "We made the *Today* show this morning, and I think I saw a CNN van drive up the street."

"We're on TV?" I wish my phone were still working so I could text Kiersten. She's always wanted to be on TV. Not like this, though.

I hurry to finish up my cereal, then change into a pair of shorts and T-shirt Mrs. Manoukian lent me and head outside. I wiggle my toes in my borrowed sneakers. There's an extra inch beyond where my toes end, but they're still better than the shoes I wore to the dance. One, two, three, four helicopters fly overhead. Two of them stay in the same place, straight up in the air from a few houses past ours. The other two roam the sky.

"Oh my God."

When you see disasters on the news, they always throw a splashy headline at what happened, like DEVASTATION IN THE MIDWEST. I wonder what they've chosen for this news story. The only words I can come up with are the kinds of words Mom and Dad don't want to hear me say. But I can get away with "Oh my God."

42

It's not just our house that's gone. With all the trees, you used to be able to see only one house at a time as you drove up my street. But not anymore. I can see past my yard to our other next-door neighbors, the McKinstrys. The top half of their house is gone, along with all the trees. Across the street, the Garcias' house is totally flattened.

With all the trees down, I can see forever in the direction the tornado went. Right across our street and down the hill behind our house.

There's a part of me that wants to cry, but the rest of me doesn't know what to do. Mr. and Mrs. Garcia are as old as my grandparents. What if they didn't get to the basement in time? The helicopters overhead—are they looking for survivors?

"Maddie!" Mom yells from over by our house—no, our *yard*. It doesn't feel right to say "house" anymore.

I run to her. "Did you check on the Garcias?"

"Everyone in our neighborhood is accounted for." She speaks so calmly.

Our neighborhood. That's all she said.

"How far did it go? The tornado? Did everyone make it?"

Mom sighs. "You know the campground, over by the lake?"

There's nowhere to hide in the campground. No basements. Just trailers and tents.

"Oh no, Mom . . ."

"I know, honey. I know. Everyone we know is okay. We need to focus on that for right now. You're okay, your friends are okay, our family is okay. We have to take things one step at a time for the next few days." She's using that tone she probably uses with patients all the time when she has to tell them something they don't want to hear.

I've been holding my breath in again. "Okay," I say, letting it out.

"First things first." Mom hands me a pair of gardening gloves. "Let's see what we can recover." I stare at the wreckage of our house strewn all over the yard. Recover what?

I slip my hands into the too-big gloves—they must be Mr. Manoukian's—and follow Mom over to our garage, which has collapsed in on itself.

"Where are the cars?"

Mom shrugs. "Somewhere under here, I'm afraid. Don't tell your dad, but if one good thing comes out of this tornado, it's the fact that I'm finally getting a new car."

"Mom!"

She turns around, holding her index finger to her lips. "Promise?"

"Promise."

· · ·

Dad passes me an open bag of chips he snagged from the Manoukians' while we break for lunch. "Find anything worth holding on to?"

"Not really, but I did find this." I pick up the painted clay elephant that I made in Mrs. Stokey's third-grade art class. "It must have been in my closet, on that shelf that was too high for me to reach." Kiersten made one, too, that day. Does she still have hers?

Dad takes it from my hand. "I always loved that guy. Mrs. Stokey sure knows how to bring out the inner artist in everyone. Anything else?"

"A lot of what I found wasn't even ours." I hand him a pile of papers, with an envelope on top. The person it was addressed to lives two towns away.

"Jeez," he says. "You know what this means?"

I shake my head.

"Your diary's going to end up in somebody else's yard. Hope you didn't write anything in it you don't want the whole world to know." Dad raises his eyebrows.

"Good thing I don't keep a diary," I lie. My palms begin to sweat a little. I kept mine tucked under my mattress, which used to be a pretty reliable hiding spot. Well, not anymore! If someone's mail from two towns over ended up in my yard, that thing could be anywhere.

Please don't end up in Avery's yard. Please don't end up in Avery's yard. Please don't end up in Avery's yard.

Dad pulls out his phone.

"Have you heard from anybody about Hank?"

He shakes his head. "You'll be the first to know, kiddo. Promise."

I try to think of a plan as a silver SUV speeds up the hill. "Can we go for a quick drive up the street?"

"In what car, Mads?"

Dad has a point.

"If someone has Hank, they'll call us. Pretty much everyone on our street knows Hank. They'll stop by with him when they have a chance. For now, let's focus on something else. I'm sure Mom could use your help."

I wonder if Dad's thinking what I'm thinking in the very back of my mind. Anyone who knows Hank would have him back here already. Hank would be sprawled out on the nicest patch of grass with his head resting on his paws, watching us dig through the mess. Hank always knew—no, Hank *knows*—how to take it easy.

Cameron runs up and tackles Dad. "Can I use the chain saw?" He looks at Dad with hopeful eyes.

"I don't think so, buddy. Chain saws are only for us tough men."

Mom clears her throat. "Ahem?"

"And super tough ladies," Dad says, extra loud.

"Hey, Maddie, can you help me with something?" Mom yells over the buzz of the chain saw.

I stuff the wrapping from my sandwich into the bag

of chips and look around for a trash can. Except, of course, there isn't one. My whole yard looks like the inside of a trash can, so I end up leaving the trash behind and jog over to Mom.

There's dirt smeared across her forehead from all the times she's wiped the hair out of her face. "Hey, sweetie," she says. "I've been looking for our photo albums all morning and I'm not having any luck at all. I think another set of eyes would help. Younger eyes."

I don't know how Mom's able to think we could actually search for something *specific* in all of this. All morning, I've just been finding what was there and deciding if it was trash or not. Most of the time, it was. Everything I found was broken or something I stopped caring about years ago, like the clay elephant.

But looking into Mom's eyes, I see something I didn't catch earlier. Maybe she was really good at hiding how she felt, at saying everything was okay, but not believing it herself.

"Okay, Mom. Sure," I say. "I'll find 'em." My voice comes out steady and clear. Like I believe it, too.

Two hours later, I haven't found the photo albums. Actually, I haven't found much of anything, not anything that counts. Nothing to make Mom happy. Side by side, we dig through the rubble: a broken dining room chair, chunks of wall, shingles from the roof. There are so many sharp things that Mom and Dad send Cammie back over to the Manoukians' house with orders to stay inside.

I wish they felt the same way about me. Instead, I'm suddenly someone who's strong enough to help them lift things. Who's careful enough to not step on nails. Who knows when to stop asking questions. Who knows the right time to be quiet. It's like I crossed over some imaginary line to the other side and became an adult.

But I want to cross back. I want to unsee the things I'm seeing.

When I lift a piece of a cabinet from the dining room, I spot the cover of a white photo album peeking out from beneath. I wipe off bits of dust and debris. It's a wedding album. Mom and Dad's? I carry it over to an empty stretch of grass and take the gardening gloves off. They're too dirty and rough for something this delicate. With my bare hands, I open the book.

The pictures inside have this reddish-gold tinge to them, and the clothes the people are wearing look super old-school. The groom's hair is crazy, all long and feathered. There's a close-up of a little girl in a frilly white dress—a flower girl? I peer at her face, trying to see if she looks familiar, but she doesn't. Her dark hair is divided into two pigtails and curled. She's wearing white gloves embroidered with tiny flowers.

But who is she?

I turn the page and find a picture of the bride and groom, with their parents on either side. At least, I think that's who they are. But I don't really know those faces either. The mothers are both wearing fur wraps over their shoulders. I flip through the pages, examining the faces of these people, waiting for something to click before I tell Mom I found one of our albums.

But nothing clicks. I don't know these people. Some stranger's album must have been blown into our yard by the tornado. That's what I'm thinking as I skim the last few pages, until I turn to the final page and find a wedding announcement. A yellowed piece of newspaper carefully cut out and glued into the album. "Announcement: Stephen Hamilton Weds Annika Johannson."

I do know these people.

Grandpa and Grandma. Mom's parents. It's their wedding album.

"Mom!" I shout. She comes running over. "I found one."

When she sees it in my hands, she starts sobbing. I've never seen Mom cry before. Not like this. Her hands shake as she takes it from me. "Oh, Maddie."

"Mom, it's okay," I say. I look for Dad—it's usually his job to make Mom feel better—but he's not coming. I don't see him anywhere and I'm not sure where he went.

Mom sits down next to me and takes her own gloves off. She rubs her bare hands over her face.

I scoot closer and wrap my arm around her. Her whole body is heaving. I rub her back, like she always does for me when I'm sick.

She finally lifts her head. "What if this is all I have of them?" Her lips quiver as she asks the question. "I should've scanned this stuff. I always said I would. All those boxes of pictures—all the photo albums in the attic. I always put things off."

A scanner wouldn't have saved them, though. Our

computer is gone, too, everything except what's in the cloud.

That's when it really hits me: *everything* is gone. Today we're going to find all that's left, and that's it. That's all we have of everything we used to have. Only what we find today.

The stuffed giraffe I won at the carnival with Kiersten last year?

Gone.

All the letters I got from my pen pal in the Netherlands?

Gone.

Cammie's and my lost teeth that I found in Mom's sock drawer when she said I could borrow a pair of socks from her that one time?

Gone.

It's all gone. The little things and the big things, the stuff with memories and the stuff we didn't even remember we had—99.9999 percent of it is gone. Gone forever.

If it isn't broken and here, it's in someone else's yard or in the woods. One mile or five miles or twenty miles away. Doesn't matter. It's not coming back to us.

The spine of the album creaks as Mom opens it. She rubs her finger against the picture of the little girl where the edge is starting to lift up. "That's my cousin Stephanie," Mom says.

"Really?"

Mom nods. "She was only three in this picture." She turns the page.

"So little."

Mom lingers on the page with Grandma and Grandpa walking down the aisle. They look so young.

"You want to know a secret?" Mom's voice is soft.

I lean into her. "Yeah."

"There was an unannounced guest at the wedding."

"Who?"

Mom points at Grandma's belly. "Me."

"Whoa." I look at the picture more closely. Grandma doesn't look pregnant at all. "Did she know? Did Grandpa?"

"I don't know," Mom says. "I never asked them."

"So, how did you know?"

"I did the math." Mom smiles. She's never told me stuff like this before.

"I found some reinforcements!" Dad shouts from across the yard. I can't quite see him yet; there's a pile of debris blocking the view.

"Cammie?" My brother undoes everything I do. Pretty much the opposite of a reinforcement. Plus, there's still lots of broken stuff.

Dad laughs. "No, not Cammie." Dad's head peeks over the pile, and then another head joins him. The second head is wearing a dirty Red Sox hat that I know all too well. It belongs to Avery.

I stand up real fast and try to wipe the sweat off my

palms and onto my shorts, but it doesn't want to go away. In fact, I think it's multiplying now that Avery's here.

"I popped over to the Manoukians' to check in on how other folks in the neighborhood were doing, and things at Avery's house were under control for the moment, so he offered to come over and help. That's pretty nice of him, huh?" Dad's looking right at me, expecting me to say something to Avery.

"Th-th-thanks," I stammer.

"I'm gonna get the chain saw going and break down some of these branches. You want to help Maddie and her mom?" Dad says to Avery.

"Sounds good," Avery says.

"You guys want to tackle the back quadrant over there?" Mom points to the part of the house where the kitchen used to be.

"Sure thing, Mrs. E."

Avery follows me over to the only area that's been pretty much untouched all day. One look at it, and anybody could see why. Shingles and plaster and brick are all jumbled together in a big mess.

"I don't even know where to start," I say.

"Maybe with this?" Avery tugs at a big piece of a wall. It's the kind of thing that before I would've left for Mom and Dad to work on, but now everything is fair game. He tries to lift it by himself, his arm muscles flexing as he pulls at it. "Can you give me a hand?"

I grab on to the other side and we both lift together, on the count of three. My legs shake from trying to lift so much weight. "Where should we put it?" I ask.

He tilts his head to the right. "Over there."

Once we get that piece out of the way, the rest is easy, and soon we can see what was hiding underneath. An ottoman from the living room, broken dishes and glasses, a stainless steel pot in perfect condition. I grab the pot and place it on the blanket in the front yard. Anything intact gets laid out on the blanket, sort of like a yard sale.

We work in unison. Team Maddie and Avery. Lifting and moving and inspecting. It's hard to talk over Dad's chain saw, so we don't. And that's okay.

There's comfort in the quiet. In the getting things done. I keep my eyes peeled for anything else that Mom might want, things passed down from Grandma and Grandpa. But I just keep finding things that would be so easy to replace. Like that pot.

After an hour, we've uncovered several more pots and pans. Everything glass has shattered, but everything metal has survived. I wish more things were made out of metal.

Everything Mom wants to find, though—the things that really matter—is on paper. So easy to break, rip, shred. To flutter away and be lost forever.

Finally, Dad takes a water break. The buzz of the chain saw is replaced by the ringing in our ears. You're probably supposed to put in earplugs for listening to that much chain-saw buzzing, but it's not like we're going to be able to find our earplugs in all of this.

There are a million questions I want to ask Avery. Did his parents hide out in his basement? Did he have to sleep on the floor last night like us? And his stuff—is it gone just like mine?

But every time I try to open my mouth and ask him a question, all I can think about is how he held my hand last night on the car ride home. How it was the only thing that made me feel less afraid.

And then I remember how he asked Gabriella to dance. So what did that hand-holding even mean?

I know what Kiersten would say if she were here. That it is definitely not the kind of question you ask a boy to his face. Maybe over text message. And even then, only if you're brave.

I pick up an armful of shingles. I'm about to place them over to the side when I see something. A glimpse of red. The shingles fall to the ground with a clatter, and I reach for the red thing. There's still something else on top of it—part of a kitchen cabinet that's been crushed by the weight of the roof. I have to move that stuff off first. I lift the last bit of wood out of the way. Can this be what I think it is?

Family Recipes, it says, embossed on the cover.

"What'd you find?" Avery stands next to me.

"A recipe book. My grandma made it."

I hand it to him so he can see. My hand zings when it hits his. It's not the same, with both of us wearing gloves. But still.

He turns the pages more carefully than I could with gloves. "Swedish meatballs, huh?"

"Her Swedish meatballs were the best," I say. "Mom makes that recipe every year on Christmas Eve, ever since . . ." It still feels weird to talk about Grandma dying, even though it happened two years ago. "She knows the recipe by heart anyway, but I think . . ." I shake my head. Tears fill my eyes and I blink them away, fast. I can't cry in front of Avery.

"I didn't realize," I finally say when I'm pretty sure I'm not going to lose it. "I didn't realize how much these little things mattered. My mom"—I lower my voice—"she was so sad when she couldn't find this stuff. There's so much more, though. I know it's lost. This could be all she has left. This and their wedding album."

Avery closes the recipe book and hands it back to me.

Mom and Dad are both talking on their cell phones as I run the recipe book over to the blanket. I'll tell Mom later.

When I return to Avery, he's already back to work, picking up the pieces of our smashed dining room table.

"Did you lose anything important?" I grab a loose table leg.

"My bedroom is upstairs," he says.

I didn't know that. But I know what their upstairs looked like last night. Obliterated.

"You know why my parents sent me over?"

I shake my head.

"Even though my house is still standing, it's not structurally sound. We can't even go in there to get stuff from the first floor until someone comes by to inspect it. My dad said that could take weeks."

"I'm sorry," I say. *Weeks.* "When you do get to go in, what's the first thing you'll look for?"

Avery shakes his head.

What a stupid question, Maddie.

Dad starts up the chain saw again and we get back into our routine. Avery takes charge, telling me what to grab and where to move it, and I do. When he concentrates hard on lifting a heavy piece of wood, his tongue sneaks out the corner of his mouth. I don't think he knows he does it. But I don't tell him.

Sweat beads around my forehead, mixing with dirt. I take off my gloves to sip some water. It's not nearly enough to quench my thirst, but there isn't exactly a working sink nearby to refill it.

Avery says something to me, but I can't hear him over the chain saw, and I'm terrible at reading lips. He motions for the water, and I hand him the bottle.

He's drinking from my water bottle. If I had a room to save the water bottle in, a drawer, any place that was all mine, I would.

"Can I finish it off?"

"Sure."

He puts the cap back on and hands the bottle back to me. He's close enough now that we can hear each other if we both shout. "I think I know what the first thing would be," he says. "My favorite baseball card. I know that sounds cheesy, but it was signed and everything."

"Which player?" I ask.

"Big Papi."

"Whoa." That thing is probably worth a lot of money.

"What about you? If there's one thing we can find today, what would it be?"

My whole body aches when I think about it. "It's more like something I don't want to find. Not here."

"What do you mean?"

"If we found him here, it would mean he's . . . dead." My voice cracks on that word.

"Hank?"

I nod.

"I thought he was over at the Manoukians' place, Maddie. I'm so sorry."

"It's my fault." I chew on my lip. "I was supposed to feed him his supper before I left for the dance, but I didn't. I couldn't find him. I didn't try hard enough. I just left." Avery is watching me so carefully as I tell him. He almost makes me lose my place in the story, the story that doesn't have an ending—not yet, anyway. "I don't know if he's out there or if he's hurt or if he's gone or if someone else took him in."

"Maybe someone nearby has him, you know? Maybe it'll just take them a few days to get in touch."

"Yeah. Maybe." But his dog tag has Dad's cell phone number on it. And Dad's cell phone works just fine.

Avery stares at me real funny. Though maybe he's not staring at me, but past me. "Whoa, Maddie. Check it out." He gestures to something behind me.

I turn to see what he's talking about. He's pointing at one of the few trees that're still standing: a pine tree, one that was about as tall as our house used to be. Tucked in between two large branches, about halfway up, is a guitar.

"Crazy," I say.

"We've been here going through all this stuff for hours, and nobody notices a guitar in a tree."

He climbs the tree to get to the guitar. Despite looking like it's lodged in there pretty good, it comes out easily. "Catch!" he says, but he lowers it down carefully, not letting go until it's securely in my hand.

"It doesn't look that bad for being stuck in a tree." I read the label on the guitar; it's a Martin.

"Did it belong to your mom or dad?" Avery asks.

I shake my head. Nobody in our house knows how to play guitar. We're not musical at all.

If some stranger's guitar can be in our tree, what does that mean for Hank?

My dog—who's such a baby that anytime we go under a bridge, he whines and ducks his head even though he's *inside* the car—could be anywhere.

Dad takes a break from clearing the fallen trees and heads over to me and Avery. "You know the McLarens from down the street? Peg and Frank?"

I shake my head.

"They live in the big pink house near the bottom of the hill." I guess I remember them a little. We used to visit all the houses on our street every time we had a school fund-raiser. The McLarens would always buy a lot of wrapping paper. "They called a few minutes ago to offer up some of their extra bedrooms."

"We're going to stay at their house? For how long?" I ask.

"It'll take a little while to work out the timetable. Mom and I are still waiting to hear back from the insurance folks."

"We're going to stay with strangers?"

"Maddie." Dad's tone turns sharper. "The McLarens aren't strangers. They're our neighbors, and they're going out on a limb here. Your mom and I are very grateful. Would you rather we blow through your college fund to stay in a hotel?"

I shake my head. "What about Grammy's house?"

Mom pipes in. "Dad and I need to be able to commute to work. Besides, Maddie, this is where we live. This is our home."

But it's not. Mom of all people should know. A home is where your stuff is. Your memories. Your life. All that's here is a mess.

"Never mind that the McLarens were extremely generous to open up their home to us," Mom says.

I don't want somebody else's home. I want mine.

"Come on, Mads." Dad squeezes my shoulders. "Peg—sorry, Mrs. McLaren—is excited to have us. She said the more the merrier. Right, hon?"

Dad's waiting for Mom to jump in, but she's not taking the bait. "It'll be an adventure," he says.

"Yeah," I say quietly. "An adventure."

It's so like Dad to try to spin it this way. To turn losing our house in a tornado into something out of a made-for-TV movie. At least Mom's not falling for it either.

"It turns out the McLarens have more extra bedrooms than they know what to do with." Dad is staring at Avery now.

Avery lays the guitar down on the ground, accidentally hitting a string in the process.

"Avery and his parents are going to be staying there for the summer, too."

I feel like I'm on that ride at the carnival where they take you to the top, hundreds of feet up in the air, and then drop you, fast, like an out-of-control elevator.

"Really?" Avery asks.

"Yup." Dad's still grinning.

My heart and my stomach are in all the wrong places. I want someone to let me off this ride I didn't sign up for, but instead Dad just told me I'm on it for the rest of the summer.

After Dad breaks the news that we'll be staying with the McLarens for the summer along with Avery's family, it's hard to think about anything else.

As Avery and I work together to move a collapsed bureau, I try to convince myself for a second that maybe it won't be so bad. Maybe in the Hallmark movie version of this summer, all it will take is spending more time together for Avery to realize that he likes *me*, not Gabriella, and that asking her to dance was a mistake.

But then when we uncover a toilet—one of the few

things the tornado didn't break—I remember that sharing a house means sharing all of those things, too.

What if Avery uses the bathroom right after me? What if he uses it after I poop? How am I ever going to poop all summer with Avery around? Can a person die from not pooping for an entire summer? It's the kind of question Cammie loves asking Mom when we're at the grocery store and everyone can hear.

I stare at the toilet. If I don't poop all summer, I will die for sure.

"Hey, Maddie, look what I found!" Avery is sitting in the tub from Mom and Dad's bathroom.

Trying to pretend that everything is all right, I flash him a thumbs-up.

I'm going to have to get undressed in the same house as Avery, too. What if he walks into the bathroom when I'm in the shower? The McLarens better have good locks on their doors.

Can you die from not bathing? I figure the smell would probably scare off Avery—and everyone else— first.

As I'm squatting down to put broken bits of glass in a bucket, somebody jumps on my back. Somebody that reeks of peanut butter and chews with his mouth wide open.

"Cammie! Personal space!"

"Sorry." He plops down on the grass an arm's length

away. He has a towel pinned to the back of his shirt that I'm just going to ignore for right now.

"There's glass all over here, so you need to be careful."

"Okay, okay. Hey, Maddie? Look what I found." He opens up his hands to show what's tucked inside. It's my Minnie Mouse watch, the one Mom and Dad got me when we went to Disney World with Grandma and Grandpa, before Grandpa stopped understanding what was going on around him and forgot who I was.

I strap it onto my wrist.

"It's broken," Cammie says.

He's right. But it's all that I have left.

"You should get a new one." Cammie twirls, his towel cape catching the air.

"I don't want a new one." I rub the crack with my fingers. The glass isn't going to fall out. It's only cracked.

"But Daddy says we're gonna get new things because all our old things are broken."

"There are some things you can't replace, Cammie."

I look past him to Mom. She understands. It's why she wants the photo albums. She doesn't want to lose the memories. Mom doesn't have a brother or a sister. She's the only keeper of her family's memories.

"You want to be a helper?" I ask Cammie.

He nods.

I point toward an area where there isn't any broken

glass. "If you pick up all the shingles and sticks over there, maybe we can help Mom find more of the photo albums. Can you do that?"

"Like a treasure hunt?"

"Exactly."

Cammie hops up and gets right to work. Avery climbs out of the tub and we work together, digging and sorting.

After a while, Mom yells over at us. "I found a bunch of stuff from your room, Mads." She points to a big pile with a purple beanbag chair. It's okay if that didn't make it. Half the beans had already fallen out before the tornado. "Can you see what you want to keep? It might rain tonight, so we'll want to bring it over to the McLarens' house."

Avery follows me to my pile.

"That's probably about how much survived from my room," he says.

I pick up my now-headless stuffed giraffe.

"That's super creepy," Avery says. "It totally defeats the purpose of having a long neck when you're missing your head."

It would be funny if it were somebody else's giraffe. But I can't muster up a laugh. This is the stuff from my room, all that's left. And it's hardly anything.

I sit down and pick through a drawer of clothes. Somehow, my bottom drawer survived, even though the rest of the dresser is missing.

"Wait, is this yours?" Avery holds up a brown leather book. My diary.

I bolt up from my spot on the ground. "Yeah."

"Is it your diary or something?"

"No," I lie. "It's not my *diary*."

He flips it open to a page in the middle. "I did so badly on the history test today. I don't know——"

I snatch it out of his hands. Part of me wants to breathe a sigh of relief that he didn't stumble on an entry about him. The other part of me wants to whack him on the head with it, *Anne of Green Gables*–style. "What's wrong with you?" I sit back down.

Avery laughs. "Hey, you're the one who said it wasn't your diary, even though it obviously is."

I glare at him. "You know, we didn't even invite you over here. I don't need your help." It comes out so much meaner than it sounded in my head.

Avery's eyes get real big. "Fine. Sorry." He stands up. "I can go over to my hou——" He stops himself from saying that word: *house*. "I thought we were friends."

Friends. There's this feeling in my stomach. It's been there all day, but it keeps morphing and I don't know how to make sense of it. Not like a punch or a kick, but like I need to let something out, like I'm keeping a secret and it's munching away on my insides.

Gregg is his friend. Naveen is his friend.

Gabriella? Is she his *friend,* too?

"Yeah, well, nobody's keeping you here."

I'm still staring down at the diary in my hand when Avery walks away.

"Maddie? Is everything all right?" Mom crouches down on the grass next to me. "Did something happen between you and Avery?"

"It's nothing," I say. But Mom lingers anyway.

I wish I could excuse myself to go to the bathroom, to have a moment just for me. I want to sit on my bed and write in my journal and have nobody bother me. Not Mom, not Dad, not Cammie, and especially not Avery.

I would let Hank in, though. He would nuzzle his head into my lap and look up at me with those eyes, like he understood everything, everything I was feeling. All he ever wanted to do was make it better.

But it doesn't matter because he's missing and there's no place anymore that's mine. And there won't be for a long, long time.

"Maddie?"

Instead of answering her, I close my eyes.

All I have is this pile of things that used to be mine, and none of them, except for the watch and maybe my diary, are the things that I want. I want my books. Not all of them. What I want is that copy of *Matilda* that Grandma read to me. The corners are permanently creased from where we stopped every night because Grandma didn't believe in bookmarks. I want the Monet poster I got at the Museum of Fine Arts when we went there on a field trip and Avery lent me money because I forgot to bring mine. I want the bunny I've had ever since I was a baby, Baba, even though it's missing an ear and I haven't slept with it since I was seven. I still want it.

Just those things. Those three things.

But I'm never going to get them back. I'm never going to get any of it back.

Mom's hand folds around mine. "You know, with all that happened last night, I'm not sure I ever asked you how the dance went."

I open up my eyes. With my free hand, I twist a piece of grass between my fingers. When I finally look up at Mom, I don't have to say anything out loud for her to understand.

Before we head over to the McLarens' house, Dad borrows Mr. Manoukian's car.

It doesn't make sense how the Manoukians have their house and their car and all their stuff, and we have nothing.

I wonder if that's what Dad is thinking, too, as he turns Mr. Manoukian's key in Mr. Manoukian's car and backs out of Mr. Manoukian's driveway.

We start up the hill. Dad rolls all the windows down. If Hank were in the backseat, he'd stick his head outside. His ears would flap in the breeze and he'd open his mouth like he was smiling.

"Hank!" I yell out the window, squinting as I look for any sign of him as we drive by our neighbors' yards, ever so slowly. With no cars behind us, we creep up the hill at ten miles per hour. The radio's off, which is weird because Dad always listens to the sports station out of Springfield. We're both listening, waiting, hoping, praying for that bark.

Dad whistles out his window. "Hank, buddy? Hey, Hank-aroo?"

"Hank? Come on, Hank!" I yell.

We call and whistle and call and stare while the chain saws buzz, buzz, buzz away.

Until we're at the end of the street, a few miles away from our house, at the stop sign. On the left side of the street, a SOLD sign creaks with the breeze at the end of the driveway at the Lewises' old house.

It's been years since they lived there—a couple of other families have lived there since—but for some reason we still call it the Lewises'. They moved to Florida not long after their dog, Nutmeg, had puppies and we adopted one of them.

I was only six and Cammie was practically a baby. Mom took me over there and let me choose which puppy to take home. I chose Hank. He wasn't the littlest or the biggest, but right in the middle, and he licked my chin when I held him. At least, that's what Mom likes to say: "Love at first lick." I don't remember getting licked by Hank. Not that time.

I wipe my eyes. "Should we turn left or right?"

Dad turns to me. "Honey . . ."

"Right?"

There's a leaf on the road in front of us. A green maple leaf, fluttering in the breeze. I don't know what's keeping it tethered to the pavement—why it won't just fly away—because it sure seems like it wants to. Better than being run over by Mr. Manoukian's car's tires.

"We need to go back, Mads. It's time to head over to the McLarens' and have some supper."

I peer deep into the forest on my right, hoping for a glimpse of Hank's golden-brown tail from behind a tree.

But our lazy Hank has never run this far in his life.

I take in a shaky breath. "Okay."

Mrs. McLaren opens the door holding an extra-fluffy calico cat in her arms. "Come in, come in." I hope she doesn't catch Cammie wrinkling his nose at the cat. "This is Snickers. He's a little shy."

I reach out to pet Snickers, but he swipes a paw at me and hisses. "Maybe more than a little," I say.

"He'll warm up to you in no time. And wait till you meet the others! You're going to be roommates, after all." Mrs. McLaren leads me up the hardwood stairs. Along the wall are pictures of her kids, two boys and a girl, back when they were little; they're all grown-up now. There's one where it looks like the heads of everyone in the family are floating in outer space. Then I realize they're actually all wearing matching navy-blue turtlenecks and that the background is also navy blue. Weird.

She points to a closed door on the right. "Now, your friend Avery is going to be staying in this room. And his parents will be staying across the hall." She opens the next door. "And here's where you and Cameron are going to stay." I cringe. Right next door to Avery?

The room has two twin beds with pink flowery quilts. Every table and bureau in the room is covered in lacy doilies. It looks like one of the cats barfed up a craft store. On the plus side, there is a flat-screen TV mounted to the wall.

Cammie runs past me and jumps on the first bed he sees. "I get to stay with Maddie!"

"Cameron," Mom says.

"Well, I'll leave you alone to get settled," Mrs. McLaren says. "You give me a holler if you need anything. And please, call me Peg."

"Okay, Peg!" Cammie says.

"Are you okay sharing a room with Cammie, honey?" Mom asks me. "I know it's a lot to ask."

I move aside one of the pillows on the bed and lie down. After all the manual labor, I'm ready to crash. "I've done it for vacation before."

"That's true. It's just . . . this is going to take a lot longer than a vacation."

"How long?"

Mom breathes out a puff of air, blowing her bangs

up. "I wish I knew. Not days or weeks, though. Probably several months if we're going to rebuild."

Months of having Avery in the room next door. The whole summer? I almost want to scream into my pillow. Not out of happiness or anger but out of everything all at once. I don't know what to feel anymore. I've done enough feeling today and yesterday. Anyway, there's cat fur on the pillow and Mom is still staring at me, waiting for a reaction.

"Months," I finally say out loud.

Mom squeezes my shoulder. "We'll get through this."

She closes the door behind her, leaving me alone with Cammie, who's lying on top of the other twin bed doing scissors kicks in the air.

"It's just like vacation. Right, Maddie?"

I get up from the bed and stare back into the mirror on top of the long bureau. Mom's right not to believe in mirrors. The person I see across from me isn't at all the person I picture in my head. There are dirt smudges all over my face from when I pushed my hair out of the way wearing the gardening gloves. Never mind the salt crusties along the side of my nose from dried-up sweat, or Mrs. Manoukian's T-shirt, which could probably fit three of me.

No wonder Avery only sees me as a friend. Why would he see me as anything else?

"Right, Maddie? Right?"

Cammie's still waiting for an answer.

Like all the adults who tell us that everything is going to be okay, I lie to him. "Right, Cammie. Just like vacation."

After dinner, Kiersten stops by with a suitcase of clothes for me to borrow. Mom says it will tide me over until we get a chance to go shopping tomorrow. Nothing I salvaged from the tornado mess exactly makes an outfit.

"Sorry it took me so long to get here. Some of the roads are closed." On the other side of Hitchcock, where Kiersten lives, everything's just fine. Like a tornado never even happened. It's like my family and Avery's—really, everyone out on Hollow Road—are living in a different world.

I lead Kiersten into my new room and shut the door. Cammie is downstairs watching TV with his new best friend, Peg, so for the first time in twenty-four hours, I have a room to myself.

"At least, you get to stay in this nice house, right?" Kiersten pulls stuff out of the suitcase: tank tops and summer dresses and shorts and, thank God, a package of new underwear.

I pick up the pair of shoes she brought, but it turns out we don't wear the same size. "They've got heated floors in the bathroom."

"Whoa," she says. "My mom said some of the other

people from your neighborhood are staying at the school. In the gym. Can you imagine? They probably haven't even cleaned up from the dance yet."

I hold up the tank dress. It's a little faded—probably not something Kiersten would have worn this summer anyway. Mom always says beggars can't be choosers. Is that us now?

"I'll turn around and close my eyes." Kiersten sits down on Cammie's bed.

I laugh. "I don't think you have to do both."

"Okay, then. I'm keeping my eyes open. So, what's this about Avery staying here?"

I slip off Mrs. Manoukian's clothes and pull the tank dress over my head. "The tornado blew the roof off his house. Everything upstairs is gone. His dad said it might be condemned, whatever that means."

"That's awful."

I would have said the same thing yesterday. Maybe I did. But now it sounds like a bunch of words, like that thing you have to say. My house is gone. All my stuff is gone. It just is. *Awful* is what happened to the people at the campground.

"He lost all his stuff, too," I say. "Nobody knows how long we're going to stay here. It's not like my mom and dad know anything about tornadoes."

"Can I turn around yet?"

I open up the package of underwear. "Just a sec."

"I can't really believe it either, you know? My mom

had the news on. Every channel is covering our town. So crazy."

"You can turn around now."

She twists around on the bed, still cross-legged. "My mom was talking about organizing a fund drive for food and clothes. You know, for the victims."

The victims. There's this weird feeling in my throat, and it doesn't go away when I swallow.

"That's a nice idea," I say. "But food and clothes are kind of easy. I mean, people can borrow from friends or go to the store to get that. I feel bad for the people that don't have a place to stay. We're lucky we have the McLarens."

Kiersten leans in toward me, lowering her voice. "And super lucky you get to stay with Avery."

"Right," I say. Super lucky I get to stay with Avery, who talked baseball with my dad and offered to play ninja turtles with Cammie, but who didn't say one thing to me at dinner.

"Have you heard from Gabriella?" Kiersten asks.

I shake my head. "She doesn't have my number."

"She asked me for it," Kiersten says. "Anyway, we were chatting last night. She was really worried about you and your house. And she feels bad about the Avery thing. What was she supposed to do? Say no?"

Yeah, I think, although part of me isn't sure how that would've worked. Would that have seemed rude? Hurt his feelings?

I remember when the lights went out in the bath-room and what Kiersten said—actually, what she didn't say. "What would you have done if Avery asked you?"

Kiersten picks a piece of cat fur off the bed and rolls it between her fingers.

"Kiersten!"

"I don't know what I would've done."

"Do you like him, too?"

"No." This time she's too quick with the reply.

"Kiersten!"

"Only a little. I can't help it! I wish I didn't. But it's . . . it's just how I feel, you know? How am I sup-posed to change how I feel?"

I shrug.

"I was going to tell you. I was. But—I mean—does it really matter? I think I like Naveen more anyway. Actually . . ." Kiersten puts together an outfit with one of those loose T-shirts and a pair of capris. "Maybe this is a sign. You and Avery, staying in the same house."

"A sign?"

Kiersten twists a strand of hair between her fingers, like she's thinking really hard. She's always the one who sees all the cosmic connections the rest of us never do. She was the first one who noticed that Mr. Cohen, the history teacher, and Ms. Roosa, the math teacher, were dating.

"I saw something online that said you never know who you truly are until you're faced with a challenge.

Maybe this is it! The hardest thing you and Avery have ever faced."

Maybe this is a sign. Me and Avery.

"I don't know. . . ."

Someone knocks on the bedroom door.

"Yeah?" I say.

Mom opens the door. "Kiersten and her mom need to get going." She takes a quick look at me. "Cute dress! Maybe we can make Kiersten our family stylist. It'd save me a lot of time."

"I'm game," says Kiersten.

I roll my eyes. Mom's never been into shopping, not like Kiersten's mom. She's still standing in the hallway, tapping her fingertips against the doorframe, while I hand back Kiersten's shoes. "Come on, girls, let's wrap it up. It's been a long day."

As we're heading down the hallway, Kiersten spies Avery's wide-open bedroom door and heads straight for it. Before I can stop her, she's dragging me in behind her.

Avery is sitting on his bed with headphones on, typing on his laptop. At least he has that since it was in his mom's car. All our computers are gone.

"Let's go," I say to Kiersten. "Your mom's waiting."

She doesn't budge. "No way. Let's see how long it takes him to realize we're standing here." She taps her foot on the ground. Quietly at first, then louder. What if he's messaging with Gabriella?

Kiersten flails her arms like a tap dancer and that finally gets his attention.

Avery slides his headphones off his ears. "What are you doing here?"

"Visiting Maddie. Hey, I'm real sorry about your house."

"Thanks."

"So, my mom and I were talking about how it sucks that we all missed out on this big thing that every sixth grader gets and, on top of that, we have this awful tornado. It's, like, welcome to seventh grade with a side of natural disaster. Anyway, she's going to call the rec center tomorrow to see if they could do something special to make up for the dance: a big pool party for our whole class."

"Sounds better than another dance," Avery says.

I'd have to get a new bathing suit. And talk Mom into finally letting me shave my legs.

"Kiersten! Maddie! Come on, girls!" Mom shouts from downstairs.

"Sorry, gotta go," Kiersten says. I wave goodbye—actually wave—at Avery. What the heck is wrong with me?

Kiersten and I head down the stairs. She makes it look so easy—just popping into Avery's room like that.

When we get to the living room, Kiersten's mom is talking with Avery's parents and mine. She gives me a squeeze. "Anytime you need a break, you just let us know. We're happy to have you come stay at Casa Wiley."

"Mom, we're not remotely Spanish." Kiersten shakes her head.

"The offer still stands," Mrs. Wiley says.

I say goodbye to Kiersten and her mom and head back upstairs.

Avery's bedroom door is propped open. I can hear him tinkering with the guitar we found in the tree. I know I should pop in and say hi and that I'm sorry for blowing up at him earlier when he was only trying to help.

But it's so much easier to walk past, right into my room, and close the door.

Through the wall I listen to him tuning the guitar.

Months, Mom said. Months.

On Monday morning, Mom's hand on my shoulder shakes me awake. "Up and at 'em, Mads."

I roll over onto my back, blinking. Sunlight peeks through the sides of the shades, still drawn. "Did I sleep through my alarm?"

"Sure did, kiddo. It woke up the rest of us, though."

"Sorry." I sit up in bed and rub at my eyes. Across the room, Cammie's bed is already empty.

"Your brother's downstairs having breakfast with Peg," Mom says. "I figured it wouldn't hurt to let you sleep in a little. Work off the exhaustion from yesterday."

Sunday was the last day to clear off anything we wanted from the site—my old house. Mom, Dad, and I were out there all day, while Cammie got to hang out here with Peg. Tough life. Well, maybe not. Peg's probably still adjusting to having a rambunctious six-year-old in her house. My arms and back ache from all the heavy lifting—and what do we have to show for it, anyway? I found the Tupperware with my winter sweaters that Mom had packed away. Whoop-de-do.

I slide my legs out from under the sheets. Mom's already dressed for work: black pants and a silky shirt with flowers on it. Did she pick those up at the store last night when she ran errands? "You're going back to work already?"

"Life goes on, even though we're not at home. I've got patients to see at the hospital, and your father has clients who expect him to get his work done. The house . . ."

As she swipes a piece of hair behind her ear, I notice that her wrist is bare. That silver watch she always wore to work is missing. She must not have found it yesterday.

"Stuff with the house will move at its own pace," Mom says. "It's not something we have a lot of control over right now. But our lives—think fast!" She tosses me a pair of Kiersten's jean shorts.

I reach out just in time to catch them.

"Our lives don't slow down. Summer marches on, right, Mads?"

I hop down from the bed. "Right."

. . .

"I've got it," I shout, almost tripping on a loose shoelace as I sprint up toward the yellow tennis ball. I reach out my racket, and the ball ricochets off it. But not across the net. Not to the other side, like it's supposed to. Instead, it hits the high metal fencing surrounding the tennis court with a clang, then falls to the ground. *Bounce, bounce, bounce.*

"Oops."

Downcourt from me, Kiersten laughs. So do Shalane and Wren, the two girls we're playing against. The two girls who are creaming us. Thank goodness it's just camp and there's nothing at stake, or I wouldn't be laughing, too.

Owen Miller, one of the counselors, jogs by, blowing his whistle. Our signal for lunch. Finally! Kiersten and I walk over to the coolers, where they've packed in all our lunch bags. I reach for the blue lunch sack Peg lent me and toss Kiersten her orange one. We head over to the picnic tables under the trees.

Kiersten and I have been going to the Hitchcock Parks-and-Rec summer camp ever since we were in second grade because our parents both work. The activities were exciting when I was eight. Trampoline day! Zumba! Learning magic tricks! But by the time we were in fifth grade, it had totally lost its cool factor.

At least, I have Kiersten with me. Everything is better with Kiersten.

She cracks open the top of her blue Gatorade and takes a big gulp. "Oh man, I still haven't told you about that movie I watched over at Gabby's house last night. It was so unbelievably scary. So there's this house in the woods, right? Except nobody can see it. Only these three friends who stumble upon it in the forest . . ."

I munch on my tuna and apple sandwich. Why didn't Kiersten and Gabby invite me to come over and watch the movie?

"That ending! I don't know how I kept my eyes open, but I did. Maybe because I was clutching Gabby's hand the whole time I was screaming." Kiersten laughs. "Maddie?"

Gabby's hand? Are they suddenly that good of friends? In my head, I see Gabby and Kiersten on the couch together, Kiersten ducking her head under a blanket during the scary parts.

"Maybe you're braver than you thought." I take another bite of my sandwich.

"Maybe." Kiersten stares past me, like she's thinking of something. "Speaking of brave . . . how's it going with Avery on the other side of the wall?" If her eyebrows were raised any higher, they'd disappear behind her bangs.

I wish I could tell Kiersten that she was right about

me and Avery. That the tornado bringing us into the same house was a sign. Or even that we were fighting and driving each other crazy, which is what always happens when two people are secretly in love.

But none of that is true.

I lean toward Kiersten so no one else at our table can hear and lower my voice. "When I went to take a shower this morning, he was in the bathroom."

"Doing . . . ?"

"I don't know! The fan was on. And I think I could hear water running. So, taking a shower, I guess? Thank God I knocked. I don't know if he locked the door or not. That would've been awkward!" I'll need to lock the door all the time when I go to the bathroom from now on. There's no way I can leave it up to chance. Avery's probably the kind of person who would knock first, but you can never be too sure.

"Okay, so you almost walked in on him in the bathroom, but what else? You've been living in the same house for more than twenty-four hours, and that's the best story you've got for me? Come on, Maddie!"

I shrug.

The truth is, since we've been in the McLarens' house, Avery and I have been sort of avoiding each other. Besides the meeting we had the first night about how we were going to share all the household responsibilities, initiated by Mr. McLaren—I mean Frank—we've kind of done our own things.

That first night, Avery and Frank devised a system for how three families were going to share one house for the summer. Shower schedules, chore charts, meal planning. Avery's mom and dad are in charge of Monday and Wednesday dinners, Peg and Frank for Tuesday and Sunday, and Mom and Dad for Thursday and Saturday. Friday night is for takeout or leftovers. Frank even has the fridge and pantry subdivided so nobody finishes someone else's milk or favorite cereal. He and Avery got everything figured out, all the way down to the DVR.

What this all means is that I know Avery's schedule by heart. Daily chore: garbage and recycling. Dishwasher duty on Monday and Wednesday. Eight-thirty morning shower. (I don't think I'll forget that again.)

It doesn't mean that we're back to talking to each other.

"Maddie, you need to be brave. Me and Gabby, we were talking about it last night and—"

"Why were you and Gabby talking about me?"

"Because you're my friend. What's so weird about that? Anyway, what Gabby said was that you can't be all freaked out about him all the time . . . like he's some magical unicorn."

I roll my eyes.

"I'm serious, Maddie. I think she's right."

I bite into a pear, juice squirting down the sides of my mouth. I wipe it away with my hand.

"He's only a magical unicorn if you treat him like one. He's a boy in your house. One who uses the bathroom like the rest of us. Just talk to him. Like normal."

Like normal. Like it's that easy. I finish off the pear and toss the core toward the nearby trash can. It misses.

Owen passes by our table, bouncing a tennis ball on his racket while walking. I'm not sure Kiersten or I could do that successfully, even if we practiced every day for an entire summer.

"Hey, Maddie. Hey, Kiersten. You ready to get back out there and serve like the pros?"

"You know we're like the polar opposite of the Williams sisters, right?" Kiersten grabs her racket, and I grab mine, so we can do our routine.

We clink in the air. "Terrible Tennis Twins!"

Owen shakes his head at the both of us.

"Hey, at least we own it," Kiersten says.

That night, right after dinner, Cammie and I take over Peg and Frank's office to work on a missing-dog flyer.

"A little lefter."

I drag the photo of Hank to the left on the monitor.

"No, more righter!" I drag it the other way.

"Stop! Stop! It's perfect."

It's actually not quite centered, but I don't tell that to Cammie. It's a missing-dog flyer, not a school project. Nobody's grading it.

Cammie sure enjoys ordering me around. He chooses the border (dog bones) and the font (I have to talk him out of Wingdings). The only things I get to do are typing the words and deciding the right spelling. Better me than Cammie. He's good with our last name, but half the time he mixes up the *m* and the *n* and writes "Canerom."

"Ready to print it?" I ask.

Cammie nods. I look for the button to turn on Peg's snazzy printer, and we both watch as our test print comes shooting out.

The image is so sharp it looks like the real Hank is staring right back at us. His tongue's the littlest bit slobbery. Not too much, though. Not like Kiersten's dog, Pepper, who's basically a saliva machine. In the picture we used from Mom's cell phone, Hank is wearing a bow around his neck. Janice and Darlene, the ladies at the fancy dog salon where Mom takes him, always put a bow on him when they're done, but it never lasts very long. Hank would go tearing through the yard, and then we'd find the bow strung up in a bush a few days later and wonder exactly how it got there.

Do Janice and Darlene even know Hank's missing? They say he's their favorite dog, and okay, maybe they say that to every dog owner, but I always believed it. And from the wag of Hank's tail while he was getting groomed, I think he believed it, too.

I'm sorry, Hank, I think, staring into his big brown

eyes. *I should have made sure you had your dinner. I should have made sure I found you before I left for the dance. I should've—*

"Maddie?"

"Yeah?"

"We're going to find him, right?"

I clear my throat and do my best job of imitating Mom, who's found a way to sound positive without making any real promises. "We're going to try."

"I miss him." Cammie's voice gets real quiet. "Sometimes before I open my eyes in the morning, I think I can smell him. And I try to pet him in my bed when I wake up in the night."

Even though the McLarens' cats would definitely go berserk if Hank appeared out of nowhere, sometimes I think I smell him, too. Or hear the jingle from his collar bell, like he's right around the corner, just out of sight.

I hug Cammie and ruffle his hair.

The thing I don't tell Cammie is that if anyone had found Hank's collar, they would have called us by now. It's been three days since the tornado and Dad has already called everyone we know. His cell phone number is listed on the dog tag, too. Dad *always* answers his phone. Even when he's driving and he's not supposed to.

We print out twenty posters to start, and I place them in a plastic zipped folder Peg gave us so they won't get

bent or crushed in Cammie's backpack, which somehow survived the tornado. Cammie and I pass through
the kitchen. Avery has his laptop out on the table. He's
playing a computer game. Again.

"Do you think Avery wants to come?" Cammie asks.

I hear Kiersten's voice in the back of my head. *Just
talk to him.* But I can't. Even though he's right there in
front of me. "I doubt it."

Peg and Frank are out on the front porch, having
their after-dinner drinks. Peg pushes up the brim of her
hat. "Where are you folks off to?"

"The library," I say.

Frank fishes into his pocket and pulls out his wallet.
"I think a book came in for me. Would you mind picking it up?"

"Sure." I take his library card and stick it in my
pocket.

Cammie and I grab bikes from the garage. There's
an old blue Schwinn that's just the right size for me.
The only bike for someone Cammie's size is a Barbie
bike, but he doesn't seem to mind. He's convinced this
Barbie is actually a Superspy Barbie, with secret ninja
powers.

I take a left up the hill.

"That's not the way to the library," Cammie shouts
from behind me.

"Just a little detour." My legs strain to bike uphill,
but we only have to go a few houses further.

I come to a stop in front of our lot. The sun is low in the sky, and the few remaining trees cast weird shadows in the bare spots of our yard.

The lot is almost completely clear. A clean slate. That's what Mom said. It makes me think of the whiteboard at school first thing in the morning. But even then, it's not really clean. There are still little black and green bits from the writing all the days before.

Building again in the same spot as our old house, it's like we get to keep the memories. Like our old house isn't truly gone.

"Mommy said I can paint my new room any color I want," Cammie says.

"Oh yeah? What color do you want, then?"

Cammie sighs. "It's a really big decision."

I turn my bike around to go down the hill. "You'll figure it out. Come on. We've got some work to do."

My fingers are clenched against the brakes the whole way down.

I follow Cammie's lead as we make our way over to the library's bulletin board. There are lots of postings for people looking to mow your lawn or babysit your kids. Somebody is looking for a tutor. Somebody wants to be a tutor. I wonder what they would say if I called both of them up and said, *Hey, I solved your problem, how about slipping me ten bucks?*

I'm putting the second pushpin into our poster when someone says, "Hey, Maddie?"

I turn around and find Gregg. He's got a sunburn on his nose and the tips of his ears, probably from the swim camp they have at the YMCA this week.

"I'm sorry about your house."

"Thanks," I say. "How did you hear?"

Cammie realizes we're done with the poster and runs off to the children's room down the hall.

"Avery." He's bouncing a little bit on the balls of his feet. "Hey, so, are you going to that pool party?"

I nod. "Kiersten put me in charge of decorations. How do you even decorate a pool?"

"Hmm," Gregg says. "I guess you could fill it with rubber ducks or something, maybe in the school colors?"

Why didn't I think of that?

"That's a good idea," I say. "Maybe you should be on the committee."

"When's the meeting?" That wasn't what I meant.

"Um, I'll have to check with Kiersten."

Gregg keeps standing there, looking at me kind of funny. Like he's staring at my nose or my eyes or some freckle on my face. Or is that just how Gregg looks when he's not talking? (When is Gregg ever not talking?) I don't know. What I do know is that my palms feel sweaty all of a sudden.

I clear my throat. "So, I actually have to go and pick up a book for the guy we're staying with."

"Oh," he says. "Well, see you around?"

"Okay. Yeah."

I'm halfway to the checkout desk when I hear Gregg calling out my name again. I turn and see him holding something in his hand. One of the slips from the missing-dog poster, with my phone number and email.

"I hope you find Hank soon."

"Me too," I say.

Two days have passed since I posted the missing-dog signs at the library, and still not one person has emailed me.

Well, that's not exactly true.

Nobody has emailed me about *Hank,* but Gregg has emailed me about a thousand different things. I wish I were exaggerating.

First, it was the video of the cat being scared of a cucumber. My mistake was writing back: *LOL. Funny one. Later! Maddie.*

That was it. Just five words, if "LOL" even is a word. But by the next time I checked my email, there were ten messages from Gregg. Actually, eleven, because while I was reading them, he sent me another one. True, most of them were links to different YouTube videos, and it wasn't like I was the only recipient, but then there were three that he sent just to me. Even though they were about the party—so really, he should've sent them to me *and* Kiersten *and* Gabriella, who Kiersten says really wants to help out—they were only addressed to me.

Hi Maddie,

New idea!!!!!!!!!!!! What if we fill the pool with goldfish? They're really cheap. I've got $25 saved up, which could buy at least a thousand goldfish. What do you say?

—the G man

Maddie,

Scratch that. Better idea! Kiddie pools filled with slushies. I can round up at least four kiddie pools from my neighborhood. Again, $25. That's gotta buy enough slushies to fill at least two pools, right? Maybe three.

—Triple G

Maddie!!!

OK, not my best idea. But I have like a thousand more. Maybe we could meet up at the library and write them all down and then you can take the best ones to your meeting.

—Gregggggggg

Meet up at the library? Just me and Gregg?

Was that . . . a date?

All I knew was that reading his emails made me super flustered, and I was pretty sure that if Avery walked into the room right then, I would die.

For the rest of the week at camp, every time I thought about telling Kiersten about Gregg's emails, I chickened out. It felt like if I said it out loud, that would make it real.

Did I really want to be the person that Gregg had a crush on? A potentially massive crush, judging by the volume of emails.

No. I didn't want to be that person.

It was easier not to say anything. *At least for now,* I told myself.

I decided I would tell Kiersten at the Fourth of July fireworks. In the dark, while the fireworks exploded over my head. No chance that anyone else would hear. It would just be the two of us.

Somehow, it always felt easier to tell the truth in the dark.

I'm not sure what's so *spectacular* about Hitchcock's Fourth of July Spectacular, the Sunday after our first week at camp. It's pretty much just everyone in town setting up their blankets on the town common to watch fireworks shoot off from the other side of Hubbard's Pond. Plus, this year it isn't even on the *fourth* of July. It's on the second.

"Maddie! Maddie!" Cammie tugs on my hand, pulling me toward one of the vendors selling glow-in-the-dark swords.

"How much are they?" I ask the teenage seller. He has a big pimple on his nose that I try not to stare at, but it's hard.

"Five dollars each . . . or two for eight."

Do I look like I'm five years old? "Just one, thanks." I pull a wad of bills out of my pocket—money from babysitting Greta and the Germ last night—and count out five.

Cammie chooses a blue sword and slices it through the air. "Hiyaa! Chaa!" In the dark, if he does it fast enough, the glowing leaves little trails. It actually looks kind of cool—not that I want my own sword, though, thank you very much.

Together we walk back over to where Mom and Dad have spread out their blanket and set up some folding chairs next to Dr. Shanahan and her family. Dr. Shanahan's son, Aiden, is right around Cammie's age, and the two of them start duking it out with their play swords. I let Mom know I'm going to meet up with Kiersten over on the other side of the bandstand, and then I'm off.

As I walk over there, I keep my eyes peeled for

Avery. And Gregg. I wonder how many emails he's sent me since I last checked ten minutes ago. Five? If only. Probably more like five million.

Someone grabs me from behind and I squeal.

"Gotcha!" Kiersten laughs. I whip around and find not just Kiersten but Gabriella, too.

"Oh, I didn't realize—" I stop myself before I actually say it out loud. That I didn't think Gabby was coming. Meeting up at the fireworks every summer is something Kiersten and I have done forever. Just us two.

They're wearing matching blue glow necklaces. Gabriella has a third in her hand. "Got this for you," she says. I pull my ponytail out of the way, and she snaps it around my neck.

It's the first time I've seen her since the night of the dance, the night everything changed. She's wearing a New England Revolution T-shirt, soccer shorts, and flip-flops, but when I blink real fast, I can almost see her the way she looked that night. Dancing with Avery. *His* hands on *her* waist.

"So, how's your summer going?" Gabriella asks.

I hesitate. *Well, let's think. I lost my house in a tornado. And you danced with Avery. So, not very well, thanks.*

Kiersten grabs my arm. "How can you resist telling her about your victory? Come on, Mads."

"Oh, that's right. I won the Most Improved Award on the last day of tennis week at camp."

"That was the day every ball she hit stayed in the court, which is basically a miracle. If you could only see us, Gabby. We might be the worst tennis players alive."

"I hope I don't leave you in my dust next year," I joke. "Could the Terrible Tennis Twins actually split?"

Gabby stares back at us, not laughing nearly as much as me and Kiersten. I guess that's the thing about inside jokes: they're not so funny from the outside. "How about you?" I ask. "How's your summer so far?"

We start heading over to where the high school football team is selling popcorn as a fund-raiser. Gabby fills me in on how she's been waking up at six every morning since school ended to go for a run. Sometimes she even runs four miles. I'm not sure I could *walk* four miles without stopping.

We get into the line for popcorn, and I spot a booth raising money for the Hitchcock Tornado Relief Fund. It's so strange, seeing the name of our town and "tornado" in the same phrase. It's been a little over a week, and I still haven't gotten used to it.

Gabby pays for a huge bag of kettle corn, and before we're out of earshot of the football players, Kiersten says, "Can you believe how cute Gregg's older brother is?"

"Which one was he?" I ask.

"The one Gabby gave the money to." Kiersten sucks in a deep breath. "Oh my gosh, I don't think I could've done it. My hand would've been shaking like crazy. Or worse—drenched in sweat."

Gabby laughs. "Kiersten, you're nuts."

"Wait—do you think Gregg's going to be that cute by the time we're in high school?" Kiersten asks.

Gabby looks at me, as if somehow I can see into the future.

"What?" I say.

"Nothing," Gabby replies. But she has this weird smile on her face.

Wait, does she think I actually like Gregg back? That I danced with him on purpose? Sure, Gregg is kinda cute. And yeah, we're friends. Gregg is friends with everybody in our grade. But Gabby wasn't here back when Gregg burped the Pledge of Allegiance on the bus ride to Plimoth Plantation! My first boyfriend cannot be Gregg.

Headed straight toward us is Mr. C. with an ice cream cone in his hand. "Hey, Kiersten, Maddie. And . . ." It takes him a second to come up with Gabby's name. "Gabriella. How's the summer treating you?"

"Good," Gabby says.

"Great," Kiersten says.

I'm the only one who stumbles over my answer. "It's . . ."

Mr. C. palms his forehead. "I'm sorry, Maddie. What kind of a question is that after what happened in your neck of the woods. How are folks doing out on Hollow Road?"

I fill him in on how the cleanup crew had taken over this week while I was at camp, clearing out the lot so the construction company could start the frame for our new home. When he asks where we're staying in the meantime, I explain how my family and Avery's are staying with the McLarens for the rest of the summer.

"Sounds like you're banding together in hard times," he says. "Good for you. I hope you and Avery aren't driving each other too crazy in that house. It's probably better in the summertime. Less to compete over."

He means the word problems in math. During the school year, he ran a contest every week, and Avery and I were always trying to outdo each other. The longer and wackier, the better.

"Yeah," I say. "Totally."

Mr. C.'s ice cream cone is dripping down his hand from too much talking and not enough eating. He licks some chocolate off the side of his hand. "Well, I don't want this thing going to waste. Enjoy the fireworks! And, Maddie, say hi to your mom and dad for me. Tell them I'm thinking of them."

"I will."

"Bye, Mr. C.," Gabriella says.

The high school marching band starts playing in the bandstand: our two-minute warning for the fireworks display. We hurry over to Kiersten's blanket and sit down as they're playing the final notes of "The Stars and Stripes Forever." Kiersten sits in the middle, with me and Gabby on either side of her. Gabby opens up the popcorn and we pass it around, stuffing our faces with our eyes to the sky, waiting for the fireworks to go off.

From across the pond, there's a hissing sound, and then they're off. First, the big circular ones. Red, white, and blue. Cammie's favorite. I plant my hands in the grass behind us and lean back.

Normally, Mom would be worried about Hank. Fireworks always made him flip out—really, any loud sounds. He startled so easily. I blink my eyes fast for a second. The little fizzy fireworks go up next, the kind you can't see at first, but then they zip and twist, shooting out in all directions. My favorite.

"So . . . have you talked to him?" Kiersten whispers into my ear.

I think of Gabby, right on the other side of Kiersten, and what Kiersten said earlier this week at camp. I can't believe she'd talk about my feelings for Avery behind my back like that.

"Not really," I say.

"Maddie." Kiersten sighs.

"I don't want to talk about it now. Can't we just watch the fireworks?"

I wish I could tell Kiersten how I really feel. About Avery, the house, Hank, Gregg . . . Starting seventh grade was supposed to be the biggest change this summer. But now it barely makes the list.

The only thing that's stayed the same is me and Kiersten. On this same blanket, like last summer, and the summer before, and the one before that, too. Our matching glow necklaces, like we're in this together. Like we can conquer anything, even seventh grade.

But now that's different, too. Sure, it's dark, but I can't pretend there isn't a third person on the other side of Kiersten.

My phone buzzes in my pocket.

Probably another email from Gregg.

I let it sit there, dig my fingers into the grass behind us, and stare up at the sky.

13

Our second week of camp is field-trip week. It's like they felt bad about making us suffer through tennis for a whole week and decided to reward us by putting us on a bus and taking us as far away from Hitchcock as we can get in an hour. Six Flags, Frisbee golf, kayaking at the state park.

The further away we get from Hitchcock, the easier it is to forget about the tornado. Each day, we settle into life at the McLarens' more and more. I even catch Cammie calling it "home."

By Friday, I've got about a dozen mosquito bites. The last day of school feels like ages ago. Kiersten and I are sitting in the rear of the bus, heading back to Hitchcock from laser tag, when I decide to finally tell her about Gregg.

I pull my phone out of my backpack and open the email thread.

Kiersten stares out the window of the bus—long rides always make her carsick—listening to music on her iPhone.

I tap her shoulder and she pulls out the earbuds.

"I have to tell you something," I say.

"You sound so serious. Did something happen?"

I shake my head and take a deep breath, my cheeks already flushing, and not from the sunburn upon sunburn this week at camp has given me. That's the weirdest thing about the emails, how they always make me blush. Even though I don't like Gregg, they still make me feel kind of . . . special, I guess, to have a boy email me that many times.

"It's about Gregg."

The tone in Kiersten's voice changes, like she's already ready to laugh. "What about Gregg?"

"You can't tell anyone," I say. "Promise. Promise you won't tell Gabby."

"Jeez, Maddie. What's your problem with Gabby?"

"I don't have a problem with Gabby," I say. Why don't I just trust Kiersten with this secret about Gregg, like how I always used to with all of my other secrets?

"Are you still mad at her about the dance?"

"No," I say, surprised by how the word comes out, how it feels like a lie.

"That was two whole weeks ago. And it's not like

they're suddenly boyfriend and girlfriend. *You're* the one who lives with him."

"I know." I'm still clutching the phone in my hand like it's some kind of weapon.

Kiersten lowers her voice, though there's no way anyone can overhear on the bus. It's so loud in here I can barely hear my own thoughts. "Anyway, so what did you want to tell me about Gregg. I swear I'll keep it a secret, whatever it is."

I hand the phone to her. "This," I say. "All of them. It's been going on for a little over a week."

Kiersten scrolls through, laughing as her thumb swipes up and up and up. "What are you going to do?"

"You think I know? Hide under a blanket until it stops? File a restraining order?"

"Nah, you don't want to get the police involved."

"Kiersten, I was *kidding*."

"Right."

Now it's real. Gregg did send me *that many* emails. I hadn't exaggerated it in my head, like I sometimes could with Avery, like that time he sat next to me on the bus after school and I was so sure it *meant* something. There's no reading between the lines here. Gregg doesn't just like me. Gregg is *obsessed*. With *me*.

"When's the last time you saw him in person?"

"Not since that day at the library. I think his family's on vacation this week, so he's not in town. But eventually I'm going to run into him. Hitchcock's small!"

"Do you think Avery knows?"

"I hope not," I say. "Do boys really talk about that stuff? Like we do?"

"Definitely not like we do." Kiersten hands me back my phone. "If I look at this screen anymore, I will barf. And no, not because of Gregg's love for you."

I glare at her and pretend to zip my lips.

"Sorry," Kiersten says. "They're sealed. I promise."

It turns out reading the emails on my phone really did make Kiersten feel like she was going to hurl, so for the rest of the bus ride back, she stares out the window while I flip through them.

We don't exactly reach a conclusion about what I should do, but I come to my own: pretend it's not happening until it goes away. That could work, right? I delete the emails, one by one. It takes the whole bus ride, but when we pull up to the rec center, they're all gone.

Not one shred of evidence of Gregg's so-called crush on me.

It's only in my head. And Kiersten's now, too.

After dinner that night, I'm lying on Mom and Dad's bed, watching a show on their TV, when my phone buzzes.

Another Gregg email.

So much for in-box zero.

But that's not what it is this time. If only. It's an email with the subject line *Lost Dog*.

My finger trembles as I click to open it.

Hello,

I saw your posting in the supermarket the other day and wanted to reach out to you. We lost our cat, Blinky, in the tornado. It's such a hard thing to lose someone you love unexpectedly. I wish you all the luck in the world in finding your Hank.

Sincerely,

Effie Holden

I let out my breath. It isn't good news or bad news. It's no news at all.

Watching TV with Mom and Peg last night, I saw a special program about the tornado. They spotlighted stories about people that lost their pets. There was one lady saying how she couldn't find her ferret. While the newscaster had the microphone in front of her mouth, one of the rescue workers discovered her ferret. She was so excited she was shaking and could barely hold on to her wiggly little guy.

"If I lost that ugly thing in the tornado, I don't think I'd be so bent out of shape," Peg said with a laugh.

But I saw Mom wipe a tear from the corner of her eye.

So what if ferrets are a little stinky and weird? That lady loved her ferret. That's what makes it a pet, and not just any old animal. Love.

When the crew cleared off our lot, filling up dumpster after dumpster with rubble once we'd finished recovering anything valuable, they double- and triple- and quadruple-checked. Hank simply wasn't there. It was like he'd vanished.

I write back to Effie, thanking her for thinking about me and Hank. I tell her how sorry I am about her cat, and then I shut down the computer for the night.

Mom and Dad are watching some lame grown-up movie downstairs with Avery's parents and Peg and Frank, and Avery is over at a friend's house, so it's just me and Cammie upstairs. Well, and the cats. It's not just Snickers. There's also Louie and Stella. None of them are all that friendly either; they're just your ordinary cats.

When I open our bedroom door, I accidentally step on one of Cammie's library books.

"Jeez, Cammie. Can't you pick up your stuff?"

"Sorry." He sticks his head out from the tent he's crouched under. Peg helped him string sheets from the bookcase to his bed to make a tent. He started sleeping underneath it in a sleeping bag, instead of in his bed. He even calls it his lair. I call it sleeping on the floor with the cats.

I know he's not going to actually pick up after

himself—he never listens to me, only to Mom and Dad—so I pick up his books one by one and stack them on the bottom shelf of the nightstand, where Peg keeps all her knitting magazines.

"Someone saw our poster and emailed me." I climb into bed and pull a sheet over myself. The McLarens don't have air-conditioning, so it gets pretty hot in our bedroom.

Cammie stands up fast, taking the sheet with him. He pulls it off his head and the whole contraption crashes to the ground. "Wait! What?" His hair sticks up from the static.

"False alarm," I say. "She lost her cat in the storm. She wanted to say she felt bad for us."

"Oh," Cammie says. "Nobody else emailed you?"

I shake my head.

"Bummer." Cammie tries to put his tent back together, but it's too hard for him, and he eventually gives up and climbs into his bed. After we both read for a while, I turn off the light.

"'Night," I say.

"'Night, Maddie."

As I lie in bed, I listen to everyone downstairs watching the movie. Peg and Frank have a little trouble hearing, so the volume is turned up super high.

I hear the front door open and footsteps on the stairs. Somebody must have just dropped off Avery. A sliver of light shines under our door, and then the bathroom fan comes on for a second. I can never figure out which switch to flip for the bathroom light either. Footsteps down the hall, and then the door closing in the room next to ours.

There's that jingle again. The Hank jingle. But I know Avery didn't bring Hank home. If he did, I'd hear his four paws tapping all over the hardwood floors, doing his little I-can't-decide-where-to-sit dance. If he did, Hank would be whimpering outside my door, begging to be let inside, to sleep on the end of my bed or Cammie's.

But the jingle is only Avery's keys.

A sticky hand presses against my shoulder as a bolt of lightning brightens the whole room.

"I'm scared." My brother wraps his hand around my arm.

I jump up in bed. The bedroom window is wide open, rain spraying all over the windowsill and onto the floor. I get up to close it. Cammie follows me, even though it's only a couple of footsteps from my bed to the window.

"It's okay," I say. "It's just a storm."

Thunder rumbles in the distance, and another flash of lightning makes Cammie's face look white as a ghost. He clutches his stuffed turtle with one hand and cuddles up against me.

"How do you know?" he asks. "How do you know it's a regular storm and not a bad one?"

"I just do," I lie, squeezing his hand.

Another lightning flash. I count in my head, waiting for the thunder. One, two, three, four . . . It rumbles right after I count to eight. It must be coming closer.

Someone knocks on our door and Cammie startles.

"Yeah?" I say.

The door creaks open. Avery stands in the doorway, wearing basketball shorts and a Dustin Pedroia T-shirt. His hair is sticking up in all directions. "I thought I heard you guys," he says. "Can I come in?"

"Okay." I smooth down my hair.

The whole room is lit up by another lightning flash and this time I've barely started the count when the thunder hits. *Boom. Rumble. Boom.* The whole house shakes.

"I'm scared," Cammie whimpers. He hops off the bed and heads for the door, still clutching his turtle. "Maybe we should go down to the basement."

I glance at Avery. Maybe we should. Just in case.

"Hold on." Avery darts past Cammie and down the hall.

"Where's he going?" Cammie asks. "Is he going to the basement?"

"I don't know," I say. "I don't think so."

I rub my fingers together, like I always do when I get nervous before a test. *Everything's going to be okay. It's only a thunderstorm.*

Lightning flashes again and there's a big crackle, like it hit a tree right outside. Or a power line. But I glance over at the clock plugged into the wall and it still works. Cammie presses up against me.

Avery comes back in with his phone and sits right next to me on the bed. "I downloaded this weather app that lets us see the storms as they move across the state. You can set it up for alerts, so you know when a storm's coming and how bad it's going to be."

Cammie walks behind us on the bed, squeezing his head in between ours to see.

"'Severe thunderstorm watch,'" I read from the screen. "What does that mean?"

"It means that there's a likelihood of severe thunderstorms," Avery says. "The kind with high winds and hail."

Likelihood, I think. Who actually says that out loud? Avery, of course. Genius Avery. "But it's not hailing," I say.

"Right," Avery says. "That's why it's only a watch. 'Watch' means it's not for sure. Only that there's a good chance. Then you have a severe thunderstorm warning. 'Warning' means it's definitely going to happen." He swipes his thumb across the screen to show a map of the state, with green and pink and purple blobs moving from left to right. "That's the radar map. So you can follow how the storm is moving."

"And that," he says, spreading his fingers to zoom in on a pink zone, "is where we are."

"Peg really likes pink," Cammie says.

Avery laughs. "Pink means thunderstorm. It doesn't have anything to do with Peg. But you're right. She really likes pink. There's so much pink in my room that sometimes when I wake up, I wonder if I've turned into Miss Piggy in the night."

Cammie giggles.

"Since when did you become such a weather guru?" I ask.

Avery hands his phone over to Cammie. "I'm not a weather guru."

"Yeah, you are. You probably even know what Doppler radar is." I've seen the weather lady explain it on TV about a dozen times and I'm still not sure *I* get it.

"Actually, Doppler radar isn't even really a weather term. It's just any radar that uses the Doppler effect to figure out velocity data about objects at a distance."

"You're officially making my brain hurt," I say. "It's called summer vacation for a reason." I mean it as a joke, but Avery doesn't smile. Maybe you're not supposed to joke with people you're barely talking to.

"So, you know when you need to go in the basement by looking at this map with all the colors?" Cammie asks.

"Pretty much. Plus, my phone sends me alerts for tornado watches and warnings."

"So, we don't have to go in the basement?" Cammie asks.

Avery shakes his head. "Not if all this data is correct."

Cammie tosses his stuffed turtle back onto his bed. "Just a normal thunderstorm, huh?"

"Yup."

Rain lashes against the window, and another bolt of lightning brightens the room. This time the thunder doesn't sound quite so loud and the walls don't feel like they're shaking. The house feels sturdy. Like it has seen hundreds, maybe thousands, of storms like this before. And it's no big deal. It will see hundreds, thousands, maybe even millions more.

"Thank you," I whisper to Avery.

He scratches his head. Maybe he realizes that his hair is totally crazy bedhead. He tries to pat it down, but then he gives up.

Now that I've calmed down about the storm, all that I can think about is that there is a boy in my bedroom. On my bed. Not just any boy. *Avery.* But it's all wrong after what happened at the dance. And worse: this is the most we've talked since we both moved in here—the most we've talked in almost two whole weeks.

Avery clears his throat and looks right at me. "You know, even with all that data, I still get scared sometimes, too."

15

"Was anyone else woken up by the storm last night?" Dad asks, pouring a glass of orange juice just as Avery comes down the stairs.

I'm about to answer when Avery beats me to it. "There was a storm?"

My mouth shuts real fast. Did I dream it all?

No. I couldn't have. Cammie and I talked about it first thing when we woke up.

"Kind of a doozy," Dad says. "Woke us up pretty good. Would've been nice to have been able to fall back to sleep." He glances at me, sitting at the table, as I shovel bite after bite of Lucky Charms into my mouth.

After I finally swallow, I say, "Guess I slept right through it."

I stare at Avery as he sits down across from me, but he doesn't look back. He empties out the Lucky Charms box into his bowl, pulls out his cell phone, and laughs at whatever he's reading like I'm not even here.

Like last night didn't even happen. Like I imagined it because I wanted it to be real.

But it was real.

By the time Avery had gone back to his room, Cammie was asleep again. He wasn't scared anymore. Me neither. So why's Avery pretending it didn't even happen?

Instead of slurping it up like I would at home, I spoon the rest of the purple milk into my mouth and carry the bowl over to the dishwasher.

Frank comes down the stairs, with Peg trailing behind him. He heads straight for the sofa and flips on the TV. "Hey, Dan, you want to check out this golf match?" On the TV screen, a little white ball rolls straight toward a hole in the ground.

Peg taps me on the shoulder. "Maddie, I picked up some new seeds from the garden center, and I'd love some company. Maybe you can fill me in on how things are going at camp?"

I look up at Dad, who's staring straight at me. He clears his throat. "Thanks for the offer, Frank. Actually, Maddie and I were about to head over to check on the guys for a little while. Maybe later, though."

He means the construction guys. Whenever he has a chance, Dad loves to stop by to see how they're progressing with our new house.

"I think I have to go with my dad," I tell Peg.

"Of course," Peg says. "Don't worry about me. I'll keep myself busy."

I glance back at Avery, who's still texting. I wonder if he's telling his friends how scared Cammie and I were last night, if that's what he's really laughing about.

When I'm in my and Cammie's room getting ready to head over to the site, I hear Avery's parents talking loudly in their room.

I pop my head out into the hallway. The door to their room is closed, but that doesn't make much of a difference. Mr. Linden has one of those loud voices that just carry no matter what.

"Things will not fall into place, Naomi. It doesn't work like that! We don't live in a fairy-tale land. The bills just keep coming. We're not going to be able to keep up with them."

"I wasn't saying—"

"No, I know *exactly* what you're saying."

"You can finally read my mind? I've been waiting my whole life for this."

I wonder if Avery can hear from down in the kitchen. He must.

Dad's sneakers squeak against the floor. He peeks his head into my room as I'm putting on my socks. Avery's parents are still going at it, but at least their voices have gotten a little quieter.

"Come on, kiddo," Dad says. "Let's give them some space."

I follow him down the hardwood stairs, almost slipping on them in my socks.

When we walk through the kitchen this time, Avery's got his headphones on. The music blasts through them, so even I can hear.

There are so many things I want to say to him I don't know where to start. Maybe with *I'm sorry*?

But I don't think Avery wants to hear anything right now, except his music.

I slide my feet into my sneakers and close the door behind me, following Dad out into the bright sunshine.

Dad pulls the rental car into our old driveway.

He stretches his arms over his head and lets out a big sigh. "Finally, I feel like I can breathe."

I know what he means. At our house, Saturday mornings were Dad's time to read the paper and drink coffee as slowly as he liked. To savor the peace and quiet, he'd say. Peace and quiet doesn't exist at the McLarens' house. At least, not with all nine of us. And that's not even counting the cats, one of which managed to pee on Dad's work shirts right after he brought them back from the dry cleaners.

"No kidding," I say, but then I wonder if that's mean. It's not like Peg is trying to drive me crazy. It's just—sometimes I want to move at my own pace in the morning. Sometimes I'm not ready to go out and garden and answer all of Peg's questions about my life right after I wake up. Maybe that's another reason Avery's always wearing headphones.

"You know, you've been a good sport about everything. I don't think your mom and I tell you that enough. It can't be easy sharing a room with your brother for the whole summer."

"It isn't," I say with a laugh.

"Well, we appreciate it. Really, kiddo."

We get out of the car and take a look at what the "guys" have accomplished this week. The construction crew finished digging out the extension to the basement and poured in the concrete. Since we have a chance to start from scratch, Dad said we could go a little bigger this time. As I stare at it, all I can think about is Avery's house, with its blue tarp still flapping in the breeze.

It's not fair that we get to build this bigger new house when Avery's parents are still waiting to see if their insurance company will come through for them.

"What do you think, Mads?"

"It looks . . . good?" I finally say.

Dad takes off his hat and stares for a while at the concrete-edged hole in the ground. When he looks at that spot, does he see our old house? Sometimes I do. It's like how every time I get a really short haircut, it feels so strange to run my fingers through my hair and have them come out way before I'm ready for them. I still expect to see my bedroom window up there, with the shade half drawn.

But if I look at the spot long enough, I feel like I can see into the future. Not for real, like I'm some fortune-teller or anything. But I can picture a new house coming up in the old one's place, like that picture book Cammie was obsessed with a few years ago, *Building Our House*. First the floor, then the walls and the roof. The siding, the pipes, the electrical wires. Trucks coming by to drop off new furniture. A rolled-up rug sticking out of the back of Mom's station wagon.

Even though there's nothing there right now, it's going to come together. Day by day, piece by piece.

"Mom has the paint chips for whenever you're ready," Dad says.

In addition to the paint chips, Mom has a bag full of bathroom tiles and wallpaper books. She's got all this stuff piled up on the desk in their bedroom at the McLarens' house. Kiersten didn't write back when I texted her about seeing a movie tonight. If she's got plans with her family this weekend, Mom and I can work on my bedroom.

"Maybe this weekend," I say.

One of the construction workers walks over in his hard hat and tough brown leather work boots. He shakes Dad's hand and then mine. "How are we doing?"

I hold my hand up to my forehead to block the sun. "Pretty good." He asks me this every time.

"Any news about your dog?"

I shake my head.

"Well, I've been keeping my eyes open." He gives me a closed-mouth smile and cracks open a can of soda. I wish he'd offer me one. "You know, my neighbor's dog is going to have puppies in a few weeks. Labradoodles. They're still looking for some buyers." He eyes my dad. "You want me to give 'em your number?"

Dad reaches into his pocket.

"No thanks," I say to the construction guy.

"I know you folks are staying down the street, but the puppy probably won't be ready to leave until September."

I shake my head. Does Dad even see me? Do his ears work?

"Thanks for thinking of us." Dad takes a business card from the construction guy. "We'd better scoot off."

Dad and I get back into the car. The black leather seats burn my legs when I sit down. Our old car never did that. "Can we put on the AC? I'm being burned alive."

"We're just going down the street," Dad says.

But I ignore him and turn it all the way up. Hot air blasts out.

"Maddie." Dad raises his voice, reaching his hand out to turn the AC off. "What did I just say?"

I roll down my window. "Why did you do it? Why'd you take his business card?"

"I was being polite." Dad backs the car out and heads down the hill toward the McLarens' house.

"But I don't want a puppy."

"I heard you," Dad says quietly.

"I want Hank." The cool air finally starts to take over, and I stop feeling like I'm slowly being cooked alive inside the car.

"We all want Hank. By the end of the summer, though, we might be glad to have another option."

"What, you think he's dead? If he's dead, where is he? Where's his tag?"

"Honey . . ."

"No. Be real."

"Madelyn, I am being real. Tornadoes are messy, messy things. We never found out who that guitar belonged to, remember?"

"Hank's not a guitar."

We pull into the McLarens' driveway. Dad turns to me as he unbuckles his seat belt. "I don't have the answers this time, Mads. I just don't."

The following Saturday, I catch a movie with Kiersten and Gabby. In the dark theater, the only sound comes from Kiersten, in the seat next to me, sucking up the last of her Sprite through a straw.

"Shhh." I nudge her. There's this eerie whistle in the movie, and I have the worst feeling something bad's about to happen with those twins. The camera pans to a monster lurking in the corner.

Kiersten shrieks, grabbing for my hand and squeezing it tight.

I'm watching with my eyes wide open. The monster on the screen doesn't even look slightly real. The CGI is totally obvious.

I look around at the other people in the theater. There's a guy that looks like Gregg's brother, with his arm around some girl who's probably his girlfriend. I can't imagine going to a movie with a boy. Having his arm around me for a whole two hours.

It still feels weird to think that Avery came into my bedroom the night of the storm. Even though for the past week he's acted like it didn't happen, I know it did. Cammie asked me to put that storm app on my phone. Sometimes, even when the weather's perfectly fine, I open it and check the forecast. Like it's proof, though I'm not sure what of.

Maybe it's only proof that Avery wanted to make sure my little brother wasn't too freaked out.

Maybe it wasn't about me at all.

When the movie ends, Gabby's dying for some fro-yo, so we head straight for the food court in the mall.

I load my vanilla fro-yo up with gummy bears and mochi and wait in line with Gabby. Her cup is overflowing. I don't know how she crammed everything in there—graham crackers, Oreos, sprinkles, granola, Reese's peanut butter cups. "Man, you weren't kidding," I say.

"Gotta enjoy my freedom." Gabby laughs. "My dad's kind of obsessed about what I eat."

"I feel you," I say. "My mom's had some healthy-food phases."

"I wish it was just a phase." Gabby places her fro-yo

127

on the scale for the cashier to weigh. "Ever since he read this article about what Olympic soccer players eat, he thinks I eat too much."

"But you're not an Olympic soccer player. Don't you run for, like, an hour every day? You can eat whatever you want."

"Yeah, you'd think? He's obsessed with it, though. One of the reasons we moved here was because the high school's soccer team is so good. My dad's convinced it'll get me a college scholarship and then after that . . ." She hands the cashier some money and takes her fro-yo off the scale.

"The Olympics? For real?"

Gabby shrugs. She swipes her spoon across the top of her concoction and pops it in her mouth.

Kiersten steps into line behind me. Her cup is topped with strawberries, blueberries, and kiwis. It looks like it could be in an ad for fro-yo, it's that perfect.

"So, I thought we could talk about the pool party," she says to me and Gabby. "I know we've been texting ideas and stuff, but we need to make some decisions. It's only three weeks away now."

"Sure," I say.

Gabby's still licking her spoon. "Okay."

We find a table in the food court—Kiersten suggests a quiet spot behind a big plant so we can focus—and once we're sitting down, she whips out a small, sparkly planner. She shows us a map she drew of the rec center and the pool, complete with measurements. (For what, I'm not sure.)

She hands me and Gabby checklists of everything we need to do between now and the day of the pool party.

"I thought the rec center was doing most of the—"

"We've got it covered." Kiersten interrupts Gabby as she uncaps her pen. "I told them we'd take care of all of the details. And we can, right?"

"But aren't they kind of used to putting on parties there?" Gabby asks.

I nod along with Gabby as I scan the list. "Forty-three things. For real? We have camp every day during the week. How are we ever going to get this done in time?"

"This is nothing," Kiersten says. "Do you know how many things are on the president's to-do list each day? We can totally get this done."

"But . . . doesn't the president have a whole staff of assistants and other people to delegate to?" I say.

Kiersten notices that her fro-yo is melting and scoops a bunch into her mouth. There's a bit of blueberry skin stuck to her tooth, but there's no way I'm telling her right now. There's no interrupting when Kiersten's in mission mode.

"Um, you've got a . . ." Gabby taps on her own tooth. I almost want to tell her, *Watch out. When Kiersten's like this, you just need to sit back and let her run the show.*

Kiersten swipes her tongue over her front tooth. "Is it gone?"

Gabby leans in for a closer look and shakes her head.

Kiersten glances over at the bathroom. "I'll be right back. While I'm gone, can you look through the to-do list and start circling the things you'll take care of?"

I can't believe it. Have the rules changed, or are things different for Gabby? I want to enjoy it—that someone else can manage to calm Kiersten down, even if I can't—but it's not that easy.

Once Kiersten's out of sight, Gabby swaps the to-do list for her fro-yo.

I pop in a few mouthfuls of my own yogurt, and a gummy bear gets stuck on my molar.

"Man, Kiersten's kind of intense about the party planning."

"You think?" I laugh.

"Forty-three things on the to-do list? I bet even the Fourth of July Spectacular doesn't have a to-do list this long."

"Definitely not." The gummy bear finally dislodges.

Gabby leans back in her chair and groans. "I'm stuffed. Do you want my last Oreo?"

I reach over to grab it out of her cup.

Across the food court, there are some boys our age, but I don't recognize any of them. They're not from Hitchcock. One of them has longer hair, and he keeps tucking it behind his ears, laughing while he talks to his friends. He's cute. Definitely the cutest out of the four of them.

I glance over the to-do list again. If I could just email Gregg this list, he'd probably take care of everything. He's got the energy for it. (And a few thousand other ideas.)

But . . . no. When I texted Kiersten to let her know he wanted to help with party planning, back before he started sending me ten billion emails a day, she said no way. She said boys always *want* to help, but they never follow through with anything.

Kiersten's probably right. If I actually emailed Gregg, he'd probably take it the wrong way and try to do all this party stuff together, just the two of us.

Sometimes it's better to leave Kiersten in charge.

I spoon through the last of my fro-yo and look back up at those boys across the way. Gabby and I both watch them, without saying another word to each other.

"You sure you're okay hanging out by yourself?" Mom asks.

The next Friday, I'm sitting on the couch downstairs with the TV muted. "You guys never have date night anymore. Don't worry about me. I'm fine."

Mom picks some white cat fur off her navy-blue dress. She glances up the stairs. "Come on, Dan! If we don't leave now, we're not going to make our reservation." She takes in a deep breath and lets it out slowly.

Dad comes down the stairs, wearing a new dress shirt. Until they lost almost all their clothes in the tornado, I didn't realize how used to my parents wearing the same clothes over and over again I was. "You know to give us a call if anything comes up," he says.

"You're not supposed to answer your phone when you're in a nice restaurant, remember?"

Dad gives me a jokey salute. "Yes, yes, Cap'n Maddie." His dress shoes *tap, tap, tap* on the hardwood floor. I unmute the television, my sign that it's time for them to go.

Miraculously, they take the hint. "Have fun, kiddo. Don't blow up the microwave," Dad says.

"Peg showed me where she keeps the fire extinguisher. I'm all set."

One final wave from Dad, and then he closes the door behind him and Mom. I listen for the sound of the car starting up. Pulling back the front curtain, I peek out at them at the end of the long driveway.

Finally!

For the entire month we've been at the McLarens' house, I haven't had the place to myself for even one second. On the weekdays, me and Cammie and Avery are off at camps or at friends' houses. And then, starting at five, the rest of the grown-ups slowly take over. My parents or Avery's (sometimes Peg and Frank, too) crowd into the kitchen to make dinner, while Avery and Cammie and I duke it out in the living room for control of the big TV.

On the weekends, it's even worse. Frank will be puttering around on his projects in the garage or watching something on the Syfy channel with Avery or making Lego castles with Cammie. And Peg is always out in the garden or baking lemon–poppy seed muffins or trying to get me to watch Lifetime movies with her. Mom's never been that big on TV—she's more of a book person—but Peg loves her TV shows, and it's sort of nice to hang out with someone her age. I didn't realize how much I've missed it since Grandma died.

Mom likes having all these extra eyes on Cammie, which, okay, I'll admit works out pretty nice for me. But it also means I can never totally be by myself. Do the things I'd do if it were just me and Cammie, like when I used to babysit for him on the weekends or a school night.

With Kiersten's family down on the Cape this weekend, it's just me. I guess I could've texted Gabby to see if she wanted to do something, but we've never done things without Kiersten. And anyway, it's sort of nice to have a little bit of time just for me.

Cammie is having a sleepover with Grammy in Rhode Island, Peg and Frank are out with friends on a boating trip, Avery's parents are out for dinner like my parents, and Avery is at Gregg's house.

Until Mom and Dad get back from dinner, it's me and the kitties. Wherever they're hiding. Really, it's just me.

I turn the TV off and hook up my iPhone to the sound system. How loud does the volume get? Does it even matter? Are the cats going to meow in protest if I turn it up too loud?

I doubt it.

I keep twisting the volume knob. Ten, twenty, thirty. Probably thirty is loud enough.

I grab the TV remote to use like a microphone and sing along with Taylor Swift, dancing around the living room. I do a little running slide in my socks on the hardwood floors. *Shwwoooooop.* It's harder to come to a stop than I thought, and I end up perilously close to the china cabinet with all of Peg's precious collectibles.

Maybe I won't be trying that again.

So what if I don't have Taylor's singing voice? Nobody's around to tell me that I'm not matching her note for note.

My favorite song comes on next and I decide it's not quite loud enough. I turn it up five more notches and hop up on the couch, flinging my hair from side to side as I sing along with Taylor about some boy who ruined everything.

I hear a thump behind me. Probably one of the cats jumping down from the counter. Stella is a twenty-pounder, the total opposite of the graceful, prissy cats they show on cat food commercials. She's bigger than some dogs I've met.

"We . . . are never ever ever ever . . . getting back together!" I finish off the song with my eyes closed 'cause that's the only way I can get close to hitting the right notes.

But when I open my eyes, I see something move at

the edge of my vision. Something way bigger than a cat.

Avery stands in the doorway.

I jump off the couch and turn down the music. My heart's beating so loud in my chest I can hear it, and not just because it's Avery. Because my Taylor Swift show was practically an exercise routine.

"How long have you been there?"

"Um, a—"

"Never mind. Don't answer that question." I realize I'm still holding the TV remote in my hand. The same TV remote I was using as a microphone not even a minute ago. I hold it against my leg as if it might meld to it and disappear.

Nope. Still there.

"So, um, how was Gregg's?" The second the question's out of my mouth, I decide I can't hold my pseudo microphone in my hand one second longer. I try to flip the remote behind me so it'll land on the couch, all casual-like.

Instead, it clunks to the floor, batteries shooting out of it and rolling toward the coffee table.

That's when I laugh. So hard I'm closing my eyes. Avery's laughing, too. And somehow that helps more than I thought it would. Like we both needed to clear the air.

I walk over to pick up the batteries, still laughing a

little. Avery collapses on the leather chair where Frank likes to sit and kicks off his sneakers.

I pop the batteries back into the TV remote, set it on the coffee table, and sit on the couch. "So, Gregg's?"

Avery shrugs. "It was all right. I mean, it was no Taylor Swift dance party. . . ."

"Ha-ha."

He takes off his hat, wrapping his hands around it to curl the brim, and then sets it on the chair's arm. And then he rubs at his eye. He's not—no, I think he is. He's crying.

Something is wrong. I've known Avery since we were little and I've never seen him cry. Not ever.

"Avery," I say, unsure what to follow it up with. I reach my hand out for his arm. It's supposed to be electric, but there's no zap when I touch Avery's skin. It's just skin. No tougher or softer than mine. The same. "What's going on?" I probably sound like my mom, but I don't know what else to say.

He picks at his thumb. I haven't seen his hand so closely all summer, but his thumb is raw and red, like he's been picking at it for a while. It's rough, like the hands of the construction workers at our new house.

"They don't understand. None of my friends. They all think everything's already gone back to normal. It's not, you know?"

I nod.

"My parents think I don't know what's going on, but I'm not an idiot."

Duh, I think. "What do you mean?"

"We might have to move," he says. "Like, leave town."

For a quick second, I get that feeling like when I looked at my house and saw only a pile of rubble. "For good?"

"Nobody wants to help us out. I mean, you know they haven't started any work on the house because there's no money, right?"

"Um . . . yeah."

He sniffs. "The insurance company, they're a bunch of jerks. They don't want to own up to it. My parents' insurance doesn't cover tornadoes. And they don't have enough money to fix the house if the insurance doesn't come through."

I swallow hard. "Where would you go?"

"Dad said we could rent, but it would have to be some place closer to where he works. Some suburb of Springfield."

"You'd have to change schools?" I think about our new house. Sure, it's not done yet, but it'll be ready for the start of school, right? And it'll be bigger. Maybe they could stay with us until they have enough money to fix their house.

Avery nods. "I've lived here my whole life, you know? I don't want to leave. I don't want to go some-

138

where new for seventh grade, start all over again where nobody knows me." His voice trembles and part of me wants to hug him, but then I think that would be weird. I don't know what he wants right now.

"Did you tell your friends?"

"I try to, but they don't listen. They don't get it, Maddie. We don't really talk about serious stuff. It's not like with you. You're the only one who understands what I'm going through."

You're the only one who understands.

I'm stuck on what he just said and what it means, but I have to say something back. "With my friends, all we ever do is talk. But I haven't really talked to them about the tornado. Or what it was like losing my house. And losing Hank."

"At least, you're getting a new house."

"I know. I'm so lucky, I know that. I just wish . . ." Thinking about it makes my eyes start to tear up. Imagining a shiny new kitchen, but without Hank's food bowl. The crumbs he always scattered on the kitchen floor. Mom kept trying and trying to find a mat that would catch his crumbs, but she just couldn't. Hank went all out at mealtime.

"Are you guys—do you think you'll get a new dog? I mean, not that you should or anything. I just wondered. . . ."

I shrug. Dad hasn't mentioned it since that day I got

mad at him for taking that man's phone number about the labradoodles.

"Too soon," Avery says. "The other day, my mom thought she'd figured out a way to make the insurance people pay. A loophole, you know, but one in our favor. And she was so happy, but then, of course, it turned out to be not true at all." Avery shakes his head. "Sometimes it feels sort of like I'm up to bat but the umpire's got some weird idea of the strike zone and I'm going to get called out no matter what I do. You know?"

I think about how, for the most part, I've been okay with losing my house, but then, every now and then, it'll just hurt—I'll go to look for something from the past and remember it's gone forever. Or think about Hank. And suddenly I'm not okay with everything that happened. Not at all. "I get what you mean."

Avery goes quiet for a moment. "Hey, do you think that carnival will still come to town at the end of the summer?"

"I don't know."

"If it comes, we should go."

"Okay," I say almost before he's finished. *You're the only one who understands.*

"It might be my last time."

I don't know what to say to that. I can't even imagine it being true.

My stomach growls and Avery looks at me like, *Is that really your stomach?*

"Do you want some mac and cheese?" I ask.

Avery stares at me. "You know how to cook?"

"No." I laugh, heading toward the kitchen. "But I'm pretty good with the microwave."

"You have enough?" He gets up to follow me.

"There's plenty."

Avery hops onto one of the barstools while I dig through the freezer drawer, looking for my frozen mac and cheese. *It's not like with you.* I keep hearing what he said in my head, and it's hard to concentrate. I almost pull out a hunk of frozen tuna instead of the mac and cheese.

I come across a container of Mom's frozen veggie dogs. "Do you want a veggie dog, too?"

"Do I want to barf?"

Now, that's more like the normal Avery.

I pry one veggie dog out of the package, heat up the skillet, and stab holes into the frozen mac and cheese with a fork.

"I didn't realize you had to kill it first," Avery says. "Isn't mac and cheese already dead?"

I laugh. "If you don't give it room to breathe while it's heating up, it explodes all over the place. Trust me, I've made that mistake before. And aren't you the scientist? Don't you know about heat expanding things?" I place the tray in the microwave and set the timer.

"Yeah, yeah, yeah."

I serve the macaroni and cheese, plus my veggie dog,

on two plates and sit down on one of the barstools next to Avery.

The second I do, he hops down from his stool. "What do you want to drink?" he asks.

"Just water."

He pours two glasses of water from the spigot on the fridge and sits back down. I take a bite of the macaroni and cheese. "How'd I do?"

"You could probably be on *Top Chef*."

"Ha-ha." I swipe a sliver of veggie dog through my mound of ketchup.

As I'm chewing, it hits me. Two people eating a meal together. Am I on a date with Avery? Suddenly swallowing becomes a lot harder. I have to gulp some water to get my veggie dog down, and then I clear my throat a few times.

"You okay?" Avery asks. "It's been a while since I Heimliched anyone."

"You've Heimliched someone before?"

"Not a real person. Just the dummy. I shot a pea across the room." He smiles at me and takes another bite of mac and cheese.

"When did you Heimlich a dummy?"

"It was in this babysitting class my mom made me take last summer. Gregg's mom signed him up, too, so, well, let's just say there were lots of peas being shot all over the room."

That sounds like Gregg, all right. I dip a bite of mac and cheese in the ketchup.

"Do you know how to do the Heimlich?" Avery asks.

I shake my head, my mouth still full of food. After I swallow, I say, "I probably should learn, though. With the tornado, I realized I'm not that prepared for any disasters. Like, we have the lockdown drills at school, and we learned to stop, drop, and roll in kindergarten, but nobody ever told us what to do if there's a tornado. Or what if someone is choking and I'm the only one there to help?"

"Totally," Avery says. "I thought I was the only one who noticed. The tornado, it made me think about all the other things I'm not prepared for. That none of us are, right?"

I don't know what to say to that, except that I get it. Somehow, not saying anything seems right, so I nod and finish the food on my plate.

When we're done eating, Avery puts the dishes in the dishwasher, since I was the one who cooked dinner. Barely, but still. I wipe down the countertop, and soon he's done.

"So, what else were you going to do tonight?" he asks.

I shrug.

"Please, no more Taylor Swift."

My ears burn at the memory of Avery catching me dancing, but I grin. "The dance party is over," I say. "Want to watch some TV?"

"Okay."

I sit down on the couch instead of the chair I usually choose when we're all watching TV and wait to see what Avery does. There are tons of seats to choose from, but if this has somehow turned into a date, then he's supposed to sit on the couch, too. But does he know that?

He sits down on the couch but chooses the cushion furthest from me.

Well, at least he still chose the couch.

I turn on the TV and start flipping through the channels. "What do you want to watch?"

"I don't care."

There must be five million channels with the McLarens' cable package. It's so quiet even with the TV on that I can hear Avery breathing all the way from the other side of the couch.

"Okay, so I said I don't care, but I actually would rather watch one thing than a little bit of everything," Avery says, smiling.

I switch to NESN, which is showing the Red Sox game. Seems easy. Not really a date thing, but at least we both like it and I don't have to choose channels anymore. "How about this?"

"Sure."

Stella strolls onto the rug in front of us and flops over on her side with a thump. She rolls onto her back and bats at her face, like we're supposed to think she's cute or something. Avery claps his hands together when one of the Red Sox players scores a run. "Woo-hoo! Yeah, Mookie!" Stella scurries out of the living room real fast.

"You scared the cat," I say.

"Stella peed on my bed the other day. Now we're even."

"Not the biggest fan of the cats, huh?"

"Are you kidding? I'm a dog person, all the way."

Avery leans in toward the TV, elbows on his knees. "Come on, Bogaerts." He's so different now, so intense and focused, but happy, too. It's like what happened earlier didn't happen at all. The upset, lost, unsure Avery I saw was just pretend. This is the real one, the one I've known forever.

But I can't forget what he said. Moving to some suburb of Springfield. Leaving our school.

This summer has been going by so fast. I used to think that was a good thing. We were getting closer and closer to moving into our new house. Closer and closer to starting seventh grade.

But maybe that means my time with Avery is going by fast, too.

Avery stands up and yelps as Dave O'Brien says, "That ball is outta here!"

Going, going, going, gone.

18

On Saturday, it's Mom who offers to drive me to Kiersten's for the planning meeting. With the pool party just two weeks away, Kiersten's been getting more and more frazzled. While we're at camp, she'll get an idea all of a sudden for something she forgot, or something we need to do differently, and dart off to write in her planner.

That's fine when it's beach day at the lake. Not so much when we're in the middle of yoga class and supposed to be doing silent meditation.

We're halfway to Kiersten's house when Mom turns down the radio. "I was just thinking how nice it is that you and Kiersten have connected with Gabriella this summer."

"Yeah."

"That's not an easy age to make a big move. Where did she come out here from, again?"

"Minnesota," I say. But then I think it's wrong. Michigan? Montana? Definitely one of those faraway *M* states.

"I bet she's glad to have found new friends so quickly."

"Uh-huh." I stare out the window as we pass by the town pool. The sign for our party is up already. As if Kiersten would let anybody forget the date. Still. It's like a second chance at the sixth-grade dance. We've earned it, right?

"It never hurts to have more friends when you head into junior high. So many changes."

Is Mom trying to say that she thinks I should be making other friends? That Kiersten's not enough?

When Mom drops me off at Kiersten's house, Gabby's already there. It makes sense—her being next door and all—but still, there's something weird about how she's always around now. Even when I'm not.

Kiersten insists we meet on the porch because her brother and his friends have taken over the living room with their video games and pizza. Even from out here, we can hear them yelling and laughing.

Kiersten turns to me. "Did your dad's work agree to donate paper plates and cups?"

"Yup," I say. "But he says he wants any leftovers back."

I scribble down on my notepad: *Remind Dad about paper plates and cups.*

Gabriella's phone starts playing a song in her pocket.

"Gabriella!" Kiersten screeches.

"Sorry. I'll put it on vibrate."

"How about silent?" Kiersten pushes the button on her phone to check the time. "It's been almost half an hour and we have literally accomplished nothing."

I glance down at my list, where, in addition to my note about reminding Dad, I also wrote: *To do.* Not *exactly* nothing.

"Calm down, Kiki," Gabriella says. *Kiki?* "We've got plenty of time till the pool party."

"*Plenty* of time?" Kiersten raises her voice. "We have two weeks. And actually, really that's more like one week. Right now we will have plates. Oh, and a few streamers because my mom had some left over from a baby shower she threw last week. This is not good enough."

More like one week?

"Why don't we have two weeks?" I ask.

Kiersten glances over at Gabriella. "Gabby invited me to go with her family on their vacation next week."

"But we have camp." Not that camp's the most exciting place to spend your summer, but still. We've done it together every year.

"I'm sorry," Gabby says. "Since my sister's bringing a friend, my mom said it was only fair if I was allowed to ask someone, too. And I asked if I could bring two friends, but—"

"It's fine." My voice comes out an octave higher than

148

normal as I think of what Mom said in the car. Going on and on about changes and how it's so nice for Gabby to have friends.

My brain jumps ahead to camp. I have some other friends there. And I get along with the counselors. But who will I sit with on the bus? We're supposed to go into Boston next week to ride the duck boats and visit the aquarium. Kiersten loves the duck boat ride.

Kiersten and Gabby are both looking at me, like they're expecting me to say something else. But what can I say? I can't change the rules Gabby's mom made. If she even made them in the first place. It's a pretty easy cop-out, actually. *My mom said . . .* I've used that excuse before. "I understand. Totally."

Kiersten bites her lip. "Okay, anyway, so we still need to figure out how to take care of the rest of the things on the list."

I stare down at my creased printout—Kiersten's list of forty-three things we need to get done before the party—but all the numbers and words run together. *First Avery, and now Kiersten.* But no. This is worse. Avery can't control moving away. It's not his choice. Kiersten's still right here, choosing Gabby over me.

"I can take care of chaperones," Gabby says. "My mom's been trying to meet a lot of the other moms in town, so I bet she'll want to help out with that."

"Great." Kiersten scribbles on her notepad. "Okay, that leaves food, games, decorations. Maddie?"

I pop my head up.

"You're doing the decorations, right?" She turns to Gabby and says, "Her mom's wicked crafty. You should see the Halloween costumes she made for us when we were little."

Dorothy and the Cowardly Lion. Peter Pan and Tinker Bell. R2-D2 and C-3PO.

"Maddie?"

I stare back at my former best friend. "Yeah?"

"You've got the decorations under control?"

All of Mom's crafting supplies—plus what she inherited from Grandma—are gone now. Destroyed. It took years to build up that closet. Maybe decades.

"We don't have any of that stuff anymore."

"But your mom could take you shopping, right? You'll get reimbursed from the PTA."

"Okay," I say. "Sure." And I add that to my list. *Buy decorations with Mom.*

Kiersten keeps assigning jobs and my fingers move the pencil across the page to write them down, but all I can think about is my house, the way it used to be. Me and Kiersten on the front steps in our dance costumes back when we both took dance classes. (It didn't last long. We were as bad at dancing as we are at tennis.) And that blue pop-up tent that Dad put on my bed for sleepovers, the one with the stars on the ceiling. We haven't fit in it for years—at least, not the two of us. We're way too big now. But back then, we'd zipper it all up and pretend we were ninja warrior zombie princesses. Like that made any sense.

But it always did. All the games we made up, they made complete sense to me and Kiersten, even if they didn't to anybody else.

"Maddie? Did you write down what I just said?"

I look up at Kiersten. "Huh?"

She peeks at my notebook. My to-do list with only two items and about a dozen doodled stars. "Have you been paying attention at all?"

"Sorry."

Kiersten's mom steps onto the porch. "You girls want any more iced tea?"

Gabriella's eyes light up. "Yes, please." Kiersten's mom says we can call her Julie but I always feel weird about that. Plus, I don't know if it's correct to call her Mrs. Wiley since she's not married to Kiersten's dad anymore.

"This meeting is officially done-zo." Kiersten criss-crosses her legs and sits back in the wicker chair.

"Maddie, how are things going with your house?" Gabby asks.

"Pretty good," I say. "They started the framing."

"How long is it supposed to take?"

I shrug. Dad said it all depends on the weather. "Hopefully, we'll be in before school starts."

"What about Avery's house?" Kiersten asks.

I wonder if I'm supposed to keep it a secret. I decide

it can't hurt to say what anyone could see driving up our street. "I'm not sure. They haven't started any construction yet."

"Maybe he can come and stay in your house once it's ready," Kiersten says, smiling.

"It's not *that* big," I say, noticing the way Gabriella is staring at a spot on the coffee table. Is it just me or does she look like she could burn a hole in it with her eyes?

"I was just kidding," Kiersten says. "I'm sure it'll all work out."

I think about what Avery told me last night. "I hope so."

"Gregg was talking up the party big-time at soccer camp last week," Gabriella says, looking right at me. "He seemed pretty psyched for it."

I glance at Kiersten. She didn't tell her, did she?

Julie comes back out with a pitcher of freshly made iced tea. "What's this I hear about a boy at camp?"

"Mom!" Kiersten says.

"Now wait a minute. Who likes Gregg?"

I shake my head, like that will make my cheeks stop turning red. "Nobody."

Julie hands me a glass of iced tea with a little blue umbrella in it. "Does nobody's name begin with an *M*?"

"Stop it, Mom. Seriously. You're such a creeper."

"I may be a grown-up now, but I was your age once."

"Yeah," Kiersten says. "In the Stone Age."

Julie laughs it off and continues to pour iced tea. "Can I tell you girls a little story?"

"Yes!" I say. Kiersten's mom always has the best stories.

"Okay, fine." Kiersten leans back in her chair with her iced tea.

"When I was your age, I went to sleepaway camp with several of my best friends. One of us—okay, it was me—had this brilliant idea. We were going to write letters back home to our crushes."

"Letters?" Kiersten asks.

"Yup. Letters. We couldn't text—no cell phones back then! Anyway, we all wrote our letters and called back home to get the boys' addresses. On mail day, we brought our letters over to the camp post office. And do you know what happened?"

I shake my head.

"All four letters were addressed to the *same* boy." She laughs and takes a sip from her iced tea. I glance over at Gabriella, but she's focused on Julie.

"So, what happened?" Gabriella asks.

"Well, Kyle Olsen got what I'm going to guess were four pretty creepy love letters in the mail a few days later."

"But what happened after? When you got back? I mean, who'd he pick?" Gabriella asks.

"None of us," Julie says. "And we were all so embarrassed, starting the day after we sent the letters, that we never dared bring it up with him." She plays with the straw in her iced tea. "You know, years later, when we were in high school, Kyle and I had become good friends, so finally I asked him what he thought when he got all those letters. He said he didn't know who to choose, and he didn't want to hurt anyone's feelings. Plus, he wasn't really ready for a girlfriend anyway."

"If the moral of this story is that we all shouldn't be fighting over Gregg, then don't worry, Mom, we aren't," Kiersten says.

"No moral to the story."

"Ooo-kay," Kiersten says.

"You girls just holler if you need anything. I'll be upstairs, avoiding the boys." Julie takes a couple of the empty glasses with her and leaves.

"Sorry about that," Kiersten says once her mom is out of earshot.

Me and Gabriella sit there quietly, and I think about what Avery said last night. How he could only talk that way to me. *Me.*

So what if he danced with Gabriella? Kiersten was right. It was just one dance. One dance, a whole month ago.

I mean, sure, Gabby must've seen Avery this summer. Not that we've talked about it. Since the dance, I haven't asked her about Avery, and she hasn't mentioned his name either. Still, she probably saw him at soccer camp last week. But they divide up the boys and the girls for almost everything, so maybe only a little.

I stare down at the date of the party, August 5, and think about last night with Avery. *You're the only one who understands.* I draw a little circle around the date, but then it turns into a heart. I go over it again and again with the pen, and everything Kiersten is saying fades into white noise.

19

It's a long week at camp without Kiersten. For the first couple of days, she texts me all the time. (As if she's the one really missing out on hiking day and the field trip to the Eric Carle Museum of Picture Book Art.) She sends pictures of the beach in Rhode Island where they're staying. The seagull that attacked Gabby's bag of chips when she left it unattended. The rope bracelet she bought for me at one of those cute shops by the beach.

It's almost like I'm there.

Not.

And then I start getting fewer texts. Fewer picture messages. She says she's used too much of her family's data plan and that she doesn't want to get in trouble.

I want to believe her.

"The maroon balloons are on sale." Mom holds a package up to show me in the party-supplies aisle at Target on Saturday afternoon. There's exactly one week until the party. Next week at this time, I'll be slathered in sunscreen and eating pizza by the pool with Kiersten. (And Gabby, I guess.)

She and Gabby are supposed to get back from Rhode Island this afternoon. Gabby texted to ask if I wanted to come over for a sleepover tonight. I've never been over to her house before, but of course I said yes. I haven't seen Kiersten in a whole week. In the summer, that's practically forever.

"Mom." I sigh. "Our colors are *red* and white, not maroon and white."

"You sure folks will be able to tell the difference?"

I reach over and grab six packages of the red balloons.

My mom's got a lot to think about, with all the stuff she's managing to get ready for our entirely new house. I probably should've shopped for this stuff online and just asked her for the credit card.

She pushes the cart down the aisle. I add a few red and white streamers to our collection of decorations.

"Is that everything on the list?" Mom asks. "You're sure you don't need some rainbow sherbet Oreos?" She points to a display of them. "Or a taco inside of a bagel inside of a calzone?"

"Maybe what we really need is a . . ." I spot a home slushie machine a few aisles away. "A watermelon-slushie-filled pool!"

"Now, that's just . . . well, probably very sticky." Mom laughs.

"Anyway, Kiersten's taking care of the snacks." I cross off the items that are already in our cart one by one until there's only one thing left. "We've got everything for the party . . . but I still need a new bathing suit."

I take over pushing the cart as we head to the clothing section and pick through the bathing suits, looking for the best patterns in my size. There's a sparkly purple bikini, so I add it to the cart.

Mom glances down at the bikini. "That's pretty grown-up."

"Mom, I'm going into *seventh* grade."

"Are you sure?" She squints as she looks at me. "I swear, two years ago you were in diapers." Mom laughs. I peek down the aisle to make sure nobody I know heard that, even though obviously it isn't true.

"Man, Mads, seventh grade! That's the ultimate boy-crazy year, if I'm remembering correctly." I keep flipping through the bathing suits, too fast to really look at them.

Mom picks a red one-piece, practically a little-kid bathing suit, and holds it up. "How about this one?"

"It's so boring."

"School colors," Mom teases.

My mom will never get it. She's not the kind of mom who's into clothes. She's not as nerdy as Dad, but . . . maybe doctors just don't have time to think about clothes. Plus, once she's at work, she has to wear that white coat over her clothes anyway. What's the point of wearing something cute if you have to cover it up?

I pick up a sporty green two-piece. "What about this one?"

Mom nods. "Try it on to make sure."

I take the bathing suit into the fitting room.

Mom waits on the other side of the door. "I'm surprised you and Kiersten didn't go shopping for the party together."

I slide the bottoms on over my underwear. No bathing suit ever looks right in the fitting room when you've got to cram your underwear into the bottoms. It looks like I've got a lumpy butt. Or worse, like I pooped my pants.

"She was with Gabby and her family all week. Remember?"

The price tag scratches my back as I put on the top.

"Oh, that's right. Sorry, hon. This week—this whole summer, really—is just flying by. Everything all right with you two?"

I open the door. "Everything's fine," I snap. "I'll see her tonight at the sleepover."

Mom tilts her head a little to the side while she looks at me.

"What?" I turn my head and twist my body to see what I look like from behind, but it's pretty impossible.

"Nothing," Mom says. "It looks nice. I like that color on you."

"Froggy green?"

"The froggiest." She smiles and looks down at her watch. "We'd better hurry up! Grammy should be back with Cammie in half an hour."

I step back into the fitting room and close the door behind me. I wad up my socks and stuff them into the top of the bathing suit, but it only looks like a fake uniboob. I sigh.

Maybe next summer.

Mom and I look at some of the lamps and bedding and then walk over to the toiletries area. As we're passing by the shaving cream, I pipe up, "Can, um, I get a razor?"

"For . . . ?"

"My legs." I stick one out for her to take a closer look. While I'm not exactly a yeti, it is true that you can see my leg hairs if you look really hard.

"You know that once you start shaving, there's no going back, right? It'll make your hair grow in even darker and thicker."

"I know. Remember that time Michaela Powers shaved her arm?"

"I do," Mom says. "And I'm glad not to be her mother. Okay, but that's it. I swear, you walk into Target with a list of five things and somehow you always come out with a full cart."

She waits patiently while I decide between all of the different packages. How are there more than twenty kinds of razors? I mean, don't they all do the same thing? I settle on a three-pack of orange, pink, and yellow ones, and then we make our way over to the checkout area. I'm scanning the candy when I hear a familiar voice a few counters away.

Gregg!

I peek real quick, and sure enough, it is him. He's in line with his older brother. Kiersten's right, his older brother is pretty cute. Real tall and with that swoopy hair that he has to brush out of his eyes.

I still haven't seen Gregg in person since that day in the library, almost a whole month ago. And I'm not ready to now. I can feel my face getting flushed just standing here and thinking of all those emails. Even though I stopped writing back, I still get a couple each day. I grab one of those trashy magazines and pretend to read it.

"Maddie, really?" I bet Mom's shaking her head at me, but I can't look up to confirm. Especially since she said my name out loud. Wait—what if Gregg heard her?

I flip the pages faster. Someone famous cheated on

her husband. Someone's too fat. Someone's too skinny. Meanwhile, I can still hear Gregg and his brother talking about the movie they just got out of.

Oooh, I always like the photos of celebrities being "just like us." There's Taylor and her cat!

"Maddie," Mom says. "Can you give me a hand here?"

No, Mom. I need to hide behind a magazine to avoid Gregg.

I sneak another quick peek at where Gregg and his brother are standing. But they're not there anymore. Did they finish checking out?

"Maddie, I can't reach the stuff in the back of the cart."

I add my bathing suit, the streamers, and the razors to the conveyor belt. "Sorry. I was a little distracted."

"A little?" Mom turns and raises her eyebrow.

I spot Gregg and his brother heading out the door to the parking lot and let out a sigh of relief.

"I think this is it!" Gabriella stands on her tippy-toes on a folding chair in her basement, her arms reaching deep into the top shelf of the closet.

"Yessssss," Kiersten says. "I've always wanted to play with a Ouija board. Promise you won't tell my mom?"

You'd think Ouija boards were made for Kiersten's

mom, they're just hokey enough, but apparently not. My mom definitely doesn't care. It's just a piece of cardboard, she'd say. I reach out my pinkie to swear on it. "Promise."

Gabriella hops off the chair, Ouija board in hand. "I wonder if there are any ghosts in the room right now," she says with a fake spooky voice.

We sit down on the carpeted floor and form a circle around the Ouija board.

"Oh, wait, I forgot the snacks! I'll be right back." Gabby jogs up the stairs, leaving me alone with Kiersten.

Kiersten pushes up her sweatshirt sleeve, revealing her pale blue rope bracelet. It's tight around her wrist and frayed. It's not the only bracelet wrapped around her wrist either. There are at least a half-dozen friendship bracelets. "Oh, I brought yours," she says. She grabs it from her duffel bag.

I slide it over my wrist. It feels so huge—way too big—until I remember it's the water that helps tighten it up. But there's no ocean here. Nothing to make it cling to my wrist like Kiersten's and Gabby's.

"So, you guys had fun?"

Kiersten nods. "Yeah, a lot of fun. Except"—she glances up the stairs—"it was a little weird. I didn't know Gabby's parents that well . . . and her dad's kind of intense."

"Like my dad?"

"Maddie, your dad is fun. I mean, he might get upset about the Red Sox a lot, but he doesn't, like, pick on everything you do."

"Did he pick on you?"

Kiersten peeks upstairs again and lowers her voice. "No, but with Gabby, he's sort of relentless. It's like she can't do anything right, which is crazy, because Gabby's amazing at so many things, you know?"

I nod, even though I don't know.

"Anyway, we had a lot of fun, but I'm still happy to be back home. Especially because it means the pool party's in one week!"

I hear Gabby's feet on the stairs. "I hope you waited for me!" She's breathless by the time she's sitting down in our circle. She lays down a plate of hummus and cut-up veggies.

"So, who wants to ask the first question?" Kiersten says.

The only fair way to decide is to rock-paper-scissors it out. Gabriella wins, bashing Kiersten's scissors with her rock, which means Kiersten gets to go second and I'll go third.

We each place two fingers on the cream-colored plastic pointer. "Is there anybody in the room with us?" Gabriella asks.

I swallow, listening for any sounds. From upstairs,

I can hear Gabriella's sister, Brianna, arguing with their mom.

And then the pointer moves, creeping closer and closer to the YES spot of the board.

"Gabby, are you moving it?" Kiersten asks.

Gabriella shakes her head.

The pointer comes to a stop over YES.

"Can you tell us your name?" Gabriella asks.

The pointer begins to move again. This time it jolts across the board to *X*. What name begins with *X*?

It jumps again. This time to *A*. Then *D*. Then . . . *H*?

Kiersten pulls her hands off the pointer. "Gabby!"

"What? It wasn't done spelling!" Gabriella's lip quivers as a smile starts to sneak out of the right half of her mouth.

"Well, if that's how you want to use *your* turn . . ." Kiersten shakes her head. "So, it's my turn now, right?"

"Sure," Gabriella says.

"No moving it this time," Kiersten says. "I'm serious." She closes her eyes and clears her throat.

"You don't have to close your eyes," Gabriella says.

"It's my question," Kiersten says. "I can do whatever I want."

"Fine. But I'm keeping my eyes open." Gabriella looks at me.

Our hands are pressed to the pointer so lightly it's hard to believe it will move at all.

"I want to know why my dad left," Kiersten says.

"You need to say it as a question," Gabriella says. "That's what the rules on the box say."

"Like you're such a big rule follower?" Kiersten jokes. "Fine." She clears her throat again. "Why did my dad leave?"

I can feel it through my fingertips. I'm not doing the moving—at least, I don't think I am—but the pointer is creeping across the board. I glance up at Gabriella, but she shakes her head. It wouldn't make sense for it to be Kiersten. She asked the question because she doesn't know. And anyway, then I'd be able to feel her pushing it, since she's right across from me.

Slowly the pointer shifts over to the letter *S* and comes to a stop.

Kiersten opens her eyes. "*S*? What does that mean?"

"It's not done yet," Gabriella says. "You have to be patient."

This time Kiersten keeps her eyes open. The pointer moves faster now, shifting over to *N* and stopping there.

"Snakes?" Gabriella asks.

Next it slides over to the letter *O*, pauses for a second, and finally comes to a stop at *W*.

"Snow," Gabriella says. "He left to get away from the snow?"

Kiersten shakes her head, and that's when I notice the tears in the corners of her eyes. "Not *the* snow," she says. "And not to get away from it either. Jessica Snow. That's Dad's girlfriend's name."

I know that Kiersten's dad has a girlfriend—Kiersten met her when she went to Florida to visit him—but I didn't know her name. I definitely didn't know her last name was Snow, and neither did my fingers. Gabriella's either.

But there is one thing I do know. Kiersten wasn't the one moving the pointer. Nobody did. That's what the tears tell me. She wouldn't ask that question if she knew the answer.

"Do you think he—I mean, did he know her before he moved to Florida?" Gabriella asks.

"He must have. I mean, why else did he move down there? I guess . . ." She stops to sniff. "Sometimes I think he went there to get away from me and Bryant and Mom."

"No way," I say. "He wouldn't."

"He must've known her before he moved there. I don't know how."

"Do you think your mom knows?" Gabriella asks.

"If she knew, she wouldn't have so many self-help books out from the library all the time." Kiersten finally lets go of the pointer to wipe her eyes. "I just wish I knew why, you know? Why we weren't enough."

"Men are dumb," Gabriella says.

Kiersten takes a deep breath, lets it out, and then looks at me. "You ready?"

We put our hands back on the edges of the pointer. Unlike Kiersten, I keep my eyes open. Even though I don't think it could be any of us moving it on purpose, I still need to see it with my own eyes to believe.

"Can I do a two-part question if the first is a yes-or-no one?"

Gabriella sighs. "Fine."

"Is there a boy out there that likes me?"

Kiersten giggles.

"Come on," I say. "It's a legitimate question. At this rate, I'm going to be sixteen before anyone ever kisses me."

"Especially if we find out that the boy who likes you lives in Zimbabwe," Kiersten says.

I stare down at the Ouija board, my fingers pressing against the pointer ever so lightly. *Come on.*

The pointer slides over toward YES.

"Phew," Gabriella says.

I take a deep breath. Okay, now it's time for the real question. "What's his name?" Just like a multiple-choice question on a test, there is only one right answer in my mind. Especially after what Avery said last weekend.

This time I close my eyes. I feel the pointer sliding across the board. It's different this time because, even with my eyes closed, I know the board now. I know where the *A* is.

But then the pointer stops. We're not there yet. I'm not ready to open my eyes.

Gabriella giggles. "Maddie, look."

And I do.

G.

It's just a plastic board game, not even a fancy wooden one, but I can't stop myself from believing it. It was right about Kiersten's dad, so it has to be right about this.

There's only one boy in our entire grade whose name begins with G.

"Maybe when we start school, you're going to meet someone whose name begins with G," Kiersten says.

I whip my hands off the pointer and plunge them deep into the pocket of my hoodie. It's just a dumb game. A dumb game that only Cammie should believe in. But I can't even convince myself.

"Come on," Gabriella says. "You don't even know what comes next."

Her hand and Kiersten's rest on the pointer, with those matching bracelets on their wrists, the pointer still fixed on the G. The emails from Gregg. Did Kiersten tell her about them while they were in Rhode Island?

"Yeah, I do." I uncross my legs and stand up before they can see the truth in my eyes, the truth only I really know. No matter what happens between me and Avery, he's never going to like me back. It's so obvious now. It's been a week since that night Avery interrupted my Taylor Swift dance party, and nothing has changed. Nothing.

And it isn't going to.

Even a dumb piece of plastic knows it.

"I need to go to the bathroom."

I disappear up the carpeted stairs and down the hallway to the bathroom Gabriella shares with her sister. The little shelf above the toilet holds fancy lotions and hair sprays and bottles with labels in French.

There's an evil part of me that wants to switch the stuff in the bottles. To see Gabriella at the pool party without her perfect hair, perfect skin, perfect everything. If Gabriella couldn't come to the pool party, maybe for once Avery would see *me*.

But I don't know which of these bottles has stuff that will make hair disappear or get all sticky. Probably none of them.

I sit down on top of the toilet seat. On the shelf next to the toilet is a clear glass container with all of Gabriella's hair thingies. Hair ties in every color and pattern—even tie-dye—and butterfly clips. The purple stretchy headband that Gabriella wears all the time. Probably her favorite. I snatch it and stretch it between my fingers like I'm playing cat's cradle.

I know what the Ouija board would say if she asked it the same question. And she knows it, too.

A for Avery.

The Ouija board doesn't tell me anything that five billion emails didn't already tell me.

I get Gregg. Gabriella gets Avery.

I close my eyes and take five deep breaths. *It's not like with you.* With each breath, my anger subsides. The Ouija board's only acting on what it knows right now.

It doesn't have to be that way, though. Maybe Avery's leaving at the end of the summer, but I still have a chance. The pool party: that's my chance. For Avery to notice me instead of Gabriella.

I'm the only one who understands him, right?

I've got my new cute bathing suit and I'm going to shave my legs. I can learn to flirt, right? I've got a week. What did Mom say when she was getting my hair ready the night of the dance? You can learn anything on YouTube.

I slip the purple headband into my pocket and head back downstairs.

The morning of the pool party, I wake up with a stabbing pain in my stomach. I roll over to check the time on the alarm clock: 4:03. Lying on my side, I curl into a ball. There. That helps a little.

What would help more would be if Hank were here. Somehow, petting him always made me feel better when I was sick.

Kiersten gets a stomachache anytime she's really, really nervous about something. Maybe that's what this is. I've never had a stomachache from being nervous, but I also never had my house blown away by a tornado before this summer either. There's a first time for everything.

Not today, I tell my stomach. I am *not* missing the pool party. I didn't spend five hours watching how-to videos about flirting on YouTube for nothing.

I rub big circles on my belly and try my hardest to fall back to sleep.

Not. Today.

When I wake up at eight-thirty, the sheets on Cammie's bed are crumpled up into a ball. He must've woken up before me. As I put on my sweatshirt, I remember the stomachache.

It's gone. Well, maybe not entirely gone. More like a dull pain, but not nearly as bad as it was in the night. Phew.

As I head down the hallway to the bathroom, the smell of pancakes wafts up the stairwell. The TV volume is turned way up. Peg must be watching one of Cammie's Saturday morning nature shows with him. Avery's door is still closed, so I guess he's sleeping in.

I take out my new yellow razor and place it on the ledge in the bathtub. Only four hours to go until the pool party. My legs are going to be the silkiest, smoothest legs there. Or I'll be sporting a few Band-Aids.

I slide off my underwear.

No!

No, no, no, no, no.

There's a brownish-red splotch inside.

"Mom!"

Nobody answers.

Kiersten got her first period in the spring. Ever since

then, I've wanted it—at least, I thought I did. But not today. My birthday, Christmas—I don't care. Any day but today.

Back in our old house, Mom showed me where she kept her pads and tampons in the bathroom closet in case it happened when she wasn't around. "Your father is hopeless," she said. "Completely hopeless when it comes to something like this."

Still sitting on the toilet, I yell again. "Mom!"

No response.

Peg's stupid TV is too loud. Mom'll never hear me with that thing blaring.

Does Mom have a spot for pads here, in Peg and Frank's bathroom? I check under the sink. Toilet paper, plunger, toilet brush, paper towels.

No pads. No tampons either, not that I have a clue how to deal with them.

There's a knock on the door.

My underwear is still around my ankles. "Mom?"

"Are you almost done?"

Shoot. It's not Mom. It's Avery.

I wish it were appendicitis, so it could just kill me now. "I'm taking a shower."

"The water's not even running yet! I just need to pee."

I dart over to the shower and turn the faucet on. "I'm already undressed," I shout back. "Go downstairs."

"Fine," Avery says.

I leave the water running in the shower and turn on

the bathroom fan. *Think, think, Maddie.* Where would someone keep pads in the bathroom? I check all the little drawers around the sink, but it's just hair stuff and extra toothbrushes and weird lotions. There's still the closet with all the towels in it. I slide the door open. *Come on, come on.*

Maybe Peg keeps this stuff well hidden. Mom's all out in the open, but then again, she's a doctor. I stick my hand down the side of the towels, feeling for a box or a plastic container, anything out of the ordinary.

But all I find is an old bottle of bubble bath.

I creak open the door and stick my head out. "Mom?"

Footsteps on the stairs. *Please be my mom. Or my dad. Even Cammie would be okay right now. Just not Avery again.*

"Maddie?"

It's Avery's mom.

"Maddie, do you need something?" Mrs. Linden asks.

I sink down to the floor, leaving the door open a tiny crack.

"Is my mom around? I kind of . . . need her help."

Tip-tap, tip-tap. Mrs. Linden must have on dress shoes. She comes to a stop on the other side of the bathroom door.

"Your mom just left to pick up the helium tank for the pool party. Is it anything I can help with?"

"Um." If I tell her, she could tell Avery, and I'd die—I'd just die. But I've seen the commercials on TV.

All that blue liquid pouring onto the fluffy white pad. If that much is going to come out of me, I need something. And fast! There's always Peg's towels, but they're white and then I'd have to find a way to clean them and then . . .

My eyes start to tear up. "Do you . . . I mean, could I borrow—well, not borrow—you're not going to want this back when I'm done with it . . ." I sound like a moron. "I need a pad. Like, for my period."

"Oh, sweetie. You hold tight, I'll be right back."

Tip-tap down the hall. A thousand years pass before she comes back to the bathroom and slips a couple of blue padded squares through the door. "Is this your first time?"

"No," I say too fast. "Actually, yeah."

"I got mine the summer before seventh grade, too."

"Oh. Cool."

Cool?

Not cool! Not cool at all!

The last thing I want to do is swap period stories with Avery's mom.

"It's pretty startling the first time, but you'll get used to it," she says. "Anyway, I'm sure you'll want to talk about this with your mom. Do you want me to let her know when she gets back?"

I can see it in my head like a TV commercial. Right as Mom opens the door, Mrs. Linden announces, so everyone can hear it, "Breaking news! Maddie got her period!" Avery squirts milk out of his nose and Cammie asks what a period is.

"Can you tell her to come see me right away?"

"Your secret's safe with me."

I open up one of the blue pouches. My *secret*? I don't think my secret is safe from anyone once I put this diapery thing in my underwear.

"I can't go."

I'm sitting on my parents' bed with the door closed. "Shhh," Mom says. "Calm down, Maddie."

"But everyone will know!" I hug my legs to my chest. The hair's all gone from them now and I'm wearing four Band-Aids. (I probably should have waited for Mom to show me how to use the razor.)

It's a total disaster. I can't go to a pool party with blood gushing out of my body. I'll turn the water red. People will think I'm dying.

Maybe if I just close my eyes, it'll go away. I'll wake up all over again and start the day without my period. It waited twelve years to start. Can't it hold off for one more day?

"If you keep your shorts on, no one will have any idea," Mom says.

"But everyone else will be in the pool! What if

someone asks me to be on their team for pool volley-ball?"

"Then you can politely decline. Say you have ath-lete's foot or something."

"Mom!"

"Or you can tell them the truth."

I press my forehead into my knees. "I can't do that."

Mom sighs. "I don't know what else to tell you, Mads. Statistically speaking, there's no way you're the only girl there who has her period today. Find some-one else who's not going in the pool and make a new friend."

A *new* friend?

Avery will definitely be going in the pool, and so will Gabriella and Kiersten, and I'll be stuck on the sidelines with the weirdos from my class who are afraid of the water. Me and all the aquaphobes. Don't they know that our bodies are 50 percent water? Or was it 90 percent?

Avery would know.

"We need to leave soon to pick up the ice."

I uncurl myself from my ball and head into my room to change into my bathing suit.

Mom was right. I should've chosen the red one.

Once we're done carrying all the decorations from our car to the rec center's pool house, Dad hops back in. He rolls down the window. "Maddie?"

Did Mom tell him about my period? The last thing I need right now is a motivational speech from my dad. I take a deep breath and shuffle over to the car.

"One more thing." Dad sticks his head out the window.

"Dad, I need to help set up. Everyone's going to be here soon."

"Just one last little piece of advice." He clears his throat. "Watch out for any blue patches in the pool."

"Dad! That's so gross. We're seventh graders. Nobody pees in the pool anymore."

"That's where you're wrong, Mads. Hard to believe,

I know, but I was a teenage boy once." He nods his head for emphasis.

A gross one, apparently.

"Bye, Dad." I wave at him and run toward the pool house, hoping nobody else heard my crazy dad.

He shouldn't have bothered. There's no reason for me to worry about pee in the pool. This will be the first pool party I can remember that I won't be going in the water.

We have a whole hour to set up for the party. Kiersten takes charge, telling me, Gabriella, Gabriella's mom, and all the other chaperones what to do. She's got a chart with stickers and everything. I can't imagine bossing grown-ups around, but Kiersten doesn't seem to mind.

"Here." She hands me a pair of orange scissors and two packages of streamers: one red, one white. "Wind these together and then string them from the fence posts."

"Yes, sir." I do a little fake salute. "I mean, ma'am."

She glances at the clock. "Go, go, go! We're running out of time!"

We have plenty of time, but I hustle over there anyway. Not following Kiersten's orders is always a bad idea. I learned that the hard way when we had a lemonade stand as first graders. Turns out lemonade is pretty sticky when it's poured over your head.

Kiersten probably isn't going to have a tantrum if things don't go as planned today, but you can never be too sure.

"Can I help?" Gabriella asks as I'm winding tape around the pole to make sure the streamer stays. It's not as easy as I thought it would be.

"Can you cut the tape?"

She stretches out a two-inch piece and hands it to me. I stick the streamer to the post. The red and white parts don't twist together as nicely as in the ones Kiersten made, but they'll have to do.

"Any news about Hank?" Gabriella asks.

It's been so long since anyone asked about him that sometimes it almost feels like everyone forgot. Like I never even had a dog in the first place. "No." I shake my head. "Nothing real. Even with all the flyers we put up."

"That stinks," Gabriella says. "Kiersten said he was a really fun dog to have around."

"Yeah." I twist another long strand of streamers and think about that time when Kiersten and I were playing dress-up and put Hank in a costume. Mom got so mad when she saw that we'd put him in a tutu and shoved his paws into my doll's ballet slippers.

"Tape?"

Gabriella hands me another piece. "Do you think you'd ever get another dog? I mean, I know it would never be the same and all. . . ."

While we continue to put up the streamers, I tell her about the construction worker with the puppy connections. "I can't imagine my brother with a puppy. Cammie'd terrorize it. Plus, I don't know if my mom would really go for it. A puppy peeing all over a brand-new house?"

"You gotta mark it as your house somehow, right?" Gabriella laughs.

"Ew! Gross! That's enough pee talk for today."

What I don't say is that I don't want a puppy. The only dog I want is Hank. I've seen the stories on the news about dogs getting separated from their owners, only to be reunited months, sometimes years, later. I haven't given up on Hank, even if everyone else has.

"Gabby!" Kiersten yells out from the other side of the pool. "I need your help!"

Gabriella hands me the tape. "You gonna manage?"

I smile. "Do I have a choice?"

Her flip-flops smack the concrete around the pool as she walks over to Kiersten. Twist, twist, twist. Tape. Repeat. As I get into a rhythm with the streamers, I keep thinking about how with Gabriella I'm sort of like a two-sided streamer. There's the white side that thinks she could be my friend, too, that maybe it could be the three of us in the fall. That maybe somehow we could all be good friends.

But then I hit the red side. And I can't get that picture out of my head of her dancing with Avery. And the real pictures, the ones Kiersten sent me. Her and Gabriella on the beach in Rhode Island without me. *Wish you were here,* she wrote.

But what if she didn't mean it? What if she had way more fun with Gabby than she does with me?

Twist, twist, twist, tape. Twist, twist, twist, tape.

The truth is, there's this other feeling, too. One that I can't get rid of. This knobby feeling in my stomach that doesn't have anything to do with my period. I stole something from Gabriella. Something right out from her house, during a sleepover she'd invited me to.

Twist, twist, twist, tape. Red, white, red.

That knobby feeling is trying to tell me something. I wish I knew what.

A car door slams in the parking lot, and that quickly, the knobby feeling evaporates. So what if I stole her cheap hair thing? Between Avery and Kiersten, it's like she's trying to steal my whole life. And starting today, with Avery, I'm going to get it back.

"Par-tay time!"

Gregg and a few of the boys who live in his neighborhood begin to form a line at the gate. "Hey, Maddie! Hey, Kiersten! Hey, Gabby!" He doesn't single me out. Maybe that's a good sign. He's wearing the most ridiculous neon-green sunglasses, the super cheap plastic ones you can get at the gas station for ninety-nine cents.

Oh man, *all* the boys are wearing them. Neon orange, neon yellow, neon pink. They look insane.

Kiersten runs over to me. "I didn't think people would show up so early. The streamers look great, but we need to put the food out."

I follow Kiersten into the pool house, where plastic grocery bags full of chips, cheese curls, cookies, granola bars, soda, and bottled water cover every surface. "Did you leave anything on the shelves in the store?"

"Come on, come on." She grabs some big plastic bowls and starts laying them out on the table. "Chips in this one, cheese curls here, and cookies in this one." She points to the smaller bowl.

"Kiersten, relax. It's just a party. It's going to be fine." I open a bag of rippled potato chips and empty them into the bowl. I snatch a few off the top and cram them in my mouth.

"Is it?" She lets out a shaky breath.

I swallow, suddenly regretting the chips. Do I have chip breath now? "It's going to be fine," I say, staring up at the perfect blue sky with the occasional puffy cloud. I lower my voice to a whisper. "At least you didn't get your period this morning."

Kiersten claps her hand over her mouth. "Wait, you did?"

I nod.

"Whoa. Crazy. You have to tell me all about it."

"Tell you all about what?" Gabriella says, picking off a cheese curl. She pops it in her mouth and licks the orange dust off her fingers.

"Nothing." I whisper to Kiersten, "I'll tell you later." Gabriella bites her lip.

"Hey, hey, hey. No climbing the fence!" Gabriella's mom yells at the boys. Gregg inches his way down the chain-link fence. The line has grown since I last looked, even though there's still ten minutes until the official start of the party.

The pool employees gather us, along with Gabriella's mom and the other chaperones, in a shady spot under the overhang to go over ground rules. No eating or drinking in the pool. No running. No "horseplay."

The lady in charge doesn't say no peeing in the pool, but I think that's a given.

"You girls ready?" Jane, the pool employee with the bright blue Speedo and the Red Sox hat, looks over at us.

I wait to see what Kiersten says.

She flashes two thumbs up.

"I do not get paid enough for this," Jane says under her breath as she opens up the gate. The chaperones stand guard behind the food as everyone runs straight toward it. So much for "no running."

"Three cookies apiece. This is a snack, not a meal," Gabriella's mom says. "Three means three! You can't possibly be entering seventh grade if you can't correctly count to three."

"Oh no! The music!" Kiersten dashes into the pool house. I follow to make sure she doesn't choose country. I love Carrie Underwood, but not the songs about trucks. We settle on a pop station.

"Ugh, this stupid dress." Kiersten pulls on the top of her terry-cloth tube dress, and that's when I notice. She and Gabriella coordinated outfits. They're both wearing the same dress, just in different colors. Kiersten's is pink and Gabriella's is purple.

"Did you and Gabriella go shopping together?"

Kiersten keeps adjusting the top of her dress over her bathing suit. "We ordered them online," she says. "Sorry. Gabby's mom had a coupon. Buy one, get one free."

A coupon. Really? She and Gabby just wanted to do their own thing, without me.

"Look, if it makes you feel any better, I'm not really sure I like it anyway." She pulls out at the top of the dress, revealing her bathing-suit top. "Maybe it would be cute if I had some water balloons."

"One of the boys would probably pop one. You'd end up lopsided."

Kiersten laughs. "True. Maybe next year, my mom will let me buy a bathing suit with padding."

"Maybe next year, we won't need padding."

When we head back out into the sunlight, it feels like more than a few minutes have passed. Our class is spread out all around the pool. Kids are sitting two or three to a lounge chair. A few stray, soggy cheese curls float in the water.

The pizza came. And went. All that's left is a few stray slices of sausage. How come no matter how many times you tweak the order, there's always too much sausage pizza and never enough cheese?

Avery's over by the snack table with Naveen. All the lessons I learned from the YouTube videos run through my head. How to stand with my shoulders back. Touch my hair. Bite my lip. Not too much, just a little. How to look at him the right way. There's a fine line between coy and crazy, the lady on the video said. It's too much, and I can't keep it all straight. I don't usually cram for tests. I study a little each night in the days leading up to the test, so I absorb what I need to know.

I grab Kiersten out of instinct. Maybe she's not my best friend for much longer, but right now she's all I have, and I need her by my side. I have to talk to him now, before everyone's in the pool and I'm stuck on the sidelines.

"Hey, Avery." I keep my shoulders back, but my voice, the one that's supposed to be confident, comes out a little too loud. *Coy, not crazy. Coy, not crazy.*

"Hey, Maddie, Kiersten," Avery says.

Kiersten starts talking to Naveen about this trip he and his parents just went on to Nantucket. It's just me and Avery. Except I don't know what to say. I just saw Avery this morning back at the house. Nothing's new except my period. And we're not going to talk about that.

I snatch a cheese curl and try to pop it in my mouth delicately, like Gabriella. "So, what do you think?" I thrust my shoulders back and try to look at him the way the lady did it in the video, but it doesn't feel right.

Avery stares back at me. "About . . . ?"

"The party," I say. *The hair! I'm supposed to touch my hair, too.* I touch my hair.

"You guys did a good job." His eyes dart to the left and right, like he's looking for someone. "What part did you do?"

I tell him about the streamers I put up with Gabby, except I leave her name out of it.

"You've got . . . um . . ." Avery wipes at his collar.

I look down at my hair and then I see it. Bright orange cheese-curl dust, all mixed in with my brown curls.

"Oh! Oh my gosh." I grab Kiersten away from Naveen. "I'll be right back," I tell Avery, and pull Kiersten into the corner.

"Why do you have cheese curls in your hair?"

I don't even know where to start. What if I tell her

and then she tells Gabby and then the two of them laugh about it? Without me.

"Can you just help me get them out?"

"Go in the pool. They'll all come out in the water."

"I can't go in the pool. Remember?"

"Oh, right." The two of us pick the cheese-curl fragments out with our fingers until we're pretty sure they're all gone.

"Why can't you tell me about it?" Kiersten squints in the sun.

"Later," I say. "I'll tell you later."

I glance back to where I left Avery, but he's gone.

"Maddie, Kiersten. Over here!" Gregg waves from his table, where there are two empty chairs.

Kiersten and I grab slices of pizza and cans of soda and head over.

Carlie-Beth bounces at the tip of the diving board.

"Yeah, Carlieeee!" one of the guys yells.

She blasts off, slipping into the water with barely a splash.

Kiersten grabs the seat further from Gregg, leaving me with the one right next to him. *Gee, thanks, Kiersten.* I slide in and start picking at my pizza.

"I've barely seen you all summer, Maddie. That's so weird," Gregg says.

"But I saw you at—" *Target,* I was about to say. More like *hid* from him at Target. That's different. "Never mind, I don't know what I'm thinking about. I guess we've been really busy getting ready for the new house." I pick a lumpy piece of sausage off my slice.

"Only sausage left, huh?" Gregg asks.

I nod.

"It's like the orange soda of pizza. Nobody's first choice."

Kiersten leans toward Gregg. "Hey, I like orange soda!"

Gregg scrunches his nose. "Then you can drink it, am I right?" He looks to me for approval.

"It's no Dr Pepper," I say, cracking open my can.

Gregg lifts his can of Dr Pepper to toast mine and slurps a sip. I wish that lady from the YouTube video gave tips on how *not* to flirt. I need to make sure Gregg's not getting the wrong message.

I sit up straight in my chair to look around. Where the heck did Gabriella go? She's not in the pool. She's not over by the food.

"Looking for somebody?" Gregg asks.

"You seen Gabriella?"

"Oh, I've seen Gabriella."

What's that supposed to mean? I glance at Kiersten, but she shrugs.

"Bow-chicka-wow-wow." Gregg bops his head as he says it.

"Okay," I say.

"Gabby and Avery went to"—he raises his fingers for air quotes—"*refill the snacks.*"

The pizza I just ate wants to make a return appearance.

"But he's not on the committee," Kiersten says.

"Maybe you should tell him yourself," Gregg says.

I turn to look back toward the snack area. Gabriella and Avery weren't there a minute ago, but there they are now. Gabriella's not even wearing her purple tube dress, but this super cute zigzag-cutout bathing suit. She keeps touching Avery's arm with her hand, and she's laughing. Laughing like there's something so funny that only the two of them know about. She doesn't need to watch videos online to figure out how to flirt. She just knows.

Refilling the snacks.

I crumple up my paper plate.

"Maddie," Kiersten says as I push my chair back. It scrapes against the concrete, but it's so loud with the music and everyone talking and laughing and having a great time—the best time—I'm the only one that hears it. And Gabriella's laughter. Even though she's across the way, I can hear it, too.

"I've gotta go to the bathroom." I toss the crumpled-up paper plate in the trash on my way. I have to walk right past them to go to the bathroom, but Gabriella doesn't even notice me—and neither does Avery. I might as well be a disintegrating cheese curl in the pool.

When I find the girls' bathroom, it's empty. It has one of those eco-friendly light switches that Mom chose for our new house. I wave my hand forever, waiting for it to turn on. *Maybe I really am invisible,* I think, but then the light crackles on, casting a creepy blue glow over the yellow tiled walls.

I sit down in the corner stall.

The door creaks open and I hear the *smack-smack* of flip-flops.

Please don't be Gabriella.

22

"Maddie?"

It isn't Gabriella, but Kiersten.

I lift my feet off the grimy floor and press them against the door. There's no way I can hold this position for long without falling into the toilet.

"Maddie, I know you're in here."

Smack-smack. I can see her flip-flops in the spot beneath the door.

Knock, knock, knock. "Maddie, come on."

My feet creep down the door. It's that or fall into the toilet, and as bad as today has been, falling into a toilet would actually make it worse.

"Did you know?" My voice sounds so small in here. Like a mouse is on the other side of the bathroom door from Kiersten. Not a person, not me. "Are they together?"

"Maddie . . ."

"No. You have to tell me. You're my best friend. You're supposed to tell me things." But the matching dresses. Another sign. "But you don't . . . you're not."

"I'm not your friend? Well, that's news to me." Kiersten sighs. "Can you just come out here so we can talk face to face like normal people?"

"No." My voice wavers. I've read about how having your period makes you cry. But that's not why tears stream down my cheeks. I wish it were that simple. That it would all go away in three to seven days.

But when my period is over, all my problems will still be there. Adding up and multiplying, growing all the time like the worst word problem ever. First no house, no Hank, having to start all over with nothing, then Kiersten ditching me for Gabriella, and now Avery, too. Avery and Gabriella. Again. It was never just that one dance.

Kiersten sticks her hand under the door.

"What the heck are you doing?"

She's got her whole arm coming through now, bending at the elbow, reaching up for the lock, but she's not even close.

"Maddie, please."

The next thing I know, she's sliding under the door, headfirst.

"Kiersten! Do you know how dirty that floor is?"

"It'll come off in the pool."

"Yeah, and everyone swimming in it will get some infectious disease, thanks to you."

I unlock the stall door while Kiersten picks herself up off the floor. She sits up on the sink. I wipe my eyes.

"So, are they? Together?"

Kiersten shrugs. "There was this pool party at Gregg's house the other weekend—"

"At Gregg's? Why wasn't I invited?"

"Don't look at me, I wasn't invited either. It was everyone who went to soccer camp together. Look, maybe it wasn't even a party. They were just hanging out. She talks to him, you know? She acts like she likes him, like she's interested."

"And I don't talk to him? Kiersten, I live with him. I talk to him all the time. I see him every day."

But it's not entirely true. There have been plenty of times when I don't talk to him, even when I want to. Times when he's sitting by himself watching TV and I go right upstairs. Or when his door is open and he's reading on his bed and I continue on to my room. I wimp out. I second-guess what I want to say. I decide it's easier just to walk away.

And what did today prove? Even when I do try to talk to him—try to flirt—it's a disaster.

"I know. I mean, *I* know you like him. But that's

195

because you told me. You tell me everything. But does Avery know?"

How could he not?

The bathroom door opens and in comes Gabriella, with her purple dress back on. She takes one quick look at me. "Maddie, what's wrong?"

I glance at Kiersten, but she doesn't answer for me. Maybe Kiersten's right. Maybe I'm supposed to say how I really feel.

"You knew I liked him," I tell Gabriella. "And you went and did it anyway."

"Did what? Wait, with Avery? Maddie, we were *talking.*"

But she wasn't just talking. She was hair-flipping and leaning into him and touching his arm, while I basically ran my cheese-curl-dust-covered fingers through my hair like a total moron.

"You like him."

"Are you still upset about the dance? Maddie, that was over a month ago. And it was just one dance. It would've been weird if I said no. And anyway, you danced with Gregg."

"But that's different!" I say, practically shouting. "You know it is. I don't *like* Gregg. I mean, he's *Gregg*!"

The bathroom door opens again but then shuts so quickly I can't see who tried to come in.

"Maddie, did you have to shout it?" Gabriella says.

I look to Kiersten for an explanation. She mouths, "Gregg."

I grab the door, and when I look down the hallway, I see Gregg's bare back, Gregg's red swim trunks, going into the men's room.

Gabriella pushes past me to leave the bathroom. "Way to go, Maddie."

23

"Maybe he didn't hear," Kiersten says, once it's just her and me again.

"Right. Maybe the earth is flat, too. And we evolved from dolphins." I splash some water on my face. Between getting mad at Gabriella and the water, I no longer look like I was in here crying. But if we don't leave soon, there will be some rumor about a bathroom emergency, starring me.

No thanks.

"Come on," I say, and Kiersten follows me back out into the bright sunshine. I sit down by the side of the pool, lightly splashing my legs in the water.

All the pool floats have been claimed. Carlie-Beth and her friends are ruling the deep end, and in the shallow end there's some kind of contest about who can hold their breath underwater the longest. One of the chaperones is keeping a close eye on that, but nobody seems to last very long. Ten, twenty seconds, tops, but that feels like forever when you're underwater.

Kiersten sits down next to me, dipping her tan legs into the water. Her toenails are painted hot pink with little neon-green polka dots. I wonder how she did that and if she'd show me. But then I think maybe Gabriella did them.

"He might be moving." I say it quietly because I think it's still a secret.

"Avery?" Kiersten whispers.

I nod. I stop kicking my feet and let them float on top of the water. It's so loud I'm not sure why we're bothering to whisper. With everyone talking and the music and the Marco Polo game in the pool, there's no way anybody could eavesdrop on us.

I tell Kiersten about the night he came back, when it was just the two of us in the McLarens' big house, and the maybe/maybe-not date. "It was so different than all the other times with him. He was different, too." I leave out the part about him crying. "It's dumb. I mean, just because we hung out and I made us mac and cheese and he told me stuff, that doesn't mean anything."

But I want it to. Want it so badly it hurts, actually hurts.

"I don't know," Kiersten says. A beach ball floats

toward us and she kicks it back. "What if you're the only one he told?"

I squint and stare up at the sky. It's so blue, even more brilliant a blue because of those big white puffy clouds. When Kiersten and I were little, we'd lie out on her lawn, gaze up at the clouds, and talk about which animals we saw in them. Galloping horses, frogs on lily pads, a giraffe taking a nap.

"I was just the person who was there."

"You think he would've told your dad if he'd come home and it was your dad dancing around to Taylor Swift?"

I laugh. "I don't think he would've told my dad."

But she's right. There were so many other people Avery could have talked to about what was going on. One of his friends. Or his mom and dad. Or Frank. Or Peg. Peg always wants to make you a cup of tea and chat.

That night, Avery told me. Said I was the only one who understood.

But I don't know anymore. Doesn't seem like he and Gabby are having a hard time understanding each other.

I stare at my toes with their bare nails and dip them just below the surface of the water.

When I finally look up, John Gallagher is headed straight toward us in his effort to find Polo. We pull our legs out of the water and clutch them to our chests.

"Maaarcooo?" he yells. His hand bangs the edge of

the pool. "Ow! What the heck?" He turns around, eyes still closed, and swims away from us.

"You want to go get a snack?" Kiersten asks.

I look toward the snack table. All I can see is the back of Gabriella's head, but I know nothing has changed. Kiersten can say whatever she wants to make me feel better, but the truth is, we're not at my house or hers. We're at the pool, where Gabriella is in her super cute bathing suit talking to Avery.

"Not really."

I bend down to pick up a paper plate under the folding table, part of post-party cleanup duty. Do any of my classmates know how to use a trash can? I pile up the plate with stray napkins and head for the least over-flowing trash can.

"I'm not sure if this is sausage or a poop." Kiersten points to a brown chunk under one of the lounge chairs.

I remember what Dad said about boys peeing in the pool on purpose. They wouldn't . . . No. Ew, ew, ew. They'd better not. "Use a paper towel. Just in case."

Kiersten walks back to the pool house. Gabriella is sitting at one of the tables, texting someone. Avery?

"Come on, Gabby. We need to clean up. My mom'll be here soon," I say.

"In a sec," she says, still looking at her phone.

I stand there, waiting for her. "Gabby . . ."

She sighs and plunks her phone down on the table. She grabs the container of cleaning wipes and heads over to the table furthest away, like she wants nothing to do with me. What reason does she have to be upset? I'm the one who's having pretty much the worst day ever, not Gabby.

She scrubs hard at the table, as if it's actually possible to get the rec center's tables clean.

"What?" I ask her.

She stops scrubbing and turns her head up at me. "What did I do now, Maddie? Huh? What is it this time? It seems like no matter what I do, you don't like me, so I don't know why I bother trying."

Kiersten comes back out from the pool house with a sponge in her hand.

"What are you talking about?" I say.

"You're mad at me because I danced with Avery. You're mad at me because Kiersten came with me to Rhode Island. You're mad at me because I kissed Avery that day at Gregg's—"

I gasp. I can't help it. She *kissed* him. That night when Avery came home and . . .

I look at Kiersten. For the shock that's supposed to spread across her face. But it's not there.

Kiersten's eyes get real wide and it almost looks like she's going to cry.

"You knew." My voice cracks as I say it.

"It's not fair, Maddie." Gabby's starting up again, and

this time there are tears in her eyes. But I don't get why. She has everything. Everything I wanted. Everything that used to be mine. "You can't dibs someone. Avery's a person. He can choose for himself. But maybe you don't get that, that people besides you have feelings. People like Gregg."

Kiersten's still standing there with that sponge in her hand. Like she's stuck. Between her former best friend and her future one.

What if you're the only one he told?

That's what she said to me, even though she knew all along. Avery never wanted to go with me to the carnival. Not just me. He probably meant to go as a group. With Gabriella. Always, always with Gabriella.

I think of the only thing I've got. The one thing I know that nobody else does. Even if it's not a hundred percent true yet. "Yeah, well, maybe it doesn't matter anymore about Avery."

"What do you mean?" Gabby asks.

"He didn't tell you?" The knobby feeling in my stomach grows as I get ready to say it. "He's moving."

Gabriella's eyes widen. She didn't count on that. So what if Avery kissed her? So what if he did and it was magical? So freaking what. Maybe it all doesn't matter anyway.

Because Avery is leaving.

That's what he told me.

Me.

Out of the corner of my eye, I see Mom's ugly green rental car pull into the parking lot, and I thank God I have a mom who is always fifteen minutes early for everything. I march past my former best friend into the pool house to get my bag and then right back out into that too-bright sun and through the gate to the car. I don't even say goodbye.

Cammie is strapped into his booster seat behind Mom. I open the back door and slide in next to him.

"You girls are finished pretty early," Mom says as I buckle myself in. "How was the party?"

I stare at a scratch on my knee. "Fine."

"Okay." Mom has to know that "fine" is never a good answer. But at least she doesn't ask any more questions. She switches the radio to NPR, which is playing some weird story about people knitting sweaters for penguins.

"Can we tell her yet?" Cammie asks Mom.

"Tell me what?"

Cammie reaches into the pocket on the back of Mom's seat and pulls something out.

"Mom saw it on the side of the road."

Hank's collar.

The bell on Hank's collar jingles as I take it from my brother's sweaty hand.

"I didn't want to tell you like this," Mom says.

I flip over the dog tag. On the back of the little metal heart is printed: HANK EVANS, Dad's cell phone number, and our address, 14 Hollow Road. The only thing that hasn't changed.

"The sun was reflecting off it," Mom says. "It caught my eye as I was driving up the hill by the Lewises' old place. I pulled over and . . ."

I clench my fist around the tag. The bell leaves an imprint on my palm.

"I'm so sorry, honey."

The reporter on the radio is done with the penguin

story. She's talking about the stock market now and I wish Mom would turn it off, turn it all off.

"Maddie?"

I can't turn to look at Cammie. I can't let him see me cry. It's the one thing I've tried so hard not to do in front of him, no matter what. So I turn my head toward the window. Stare out at the million green leaves on the trees as we speed by. In this part of town, the trees stand tall and full of life. Not like the marching skeletons that survived the tornado in my neighborhood. Gangly and dead-looking, but somehow still standing, still haunting us. Reminding us of everything we lost.

I prefer the trees that lay down and gave up. Let the tornado take them.

Up ahead is a big field, a gap in the trees, and when we pass it, I can see the sky again. All those big, puffy clouds. I try to make out a dog in them, but it's useless.

They're just clouds.

When we get back to the McLarens' house, I'm out of the car before anyone else.

"Maddie?" Mom fiddles with the seat belt stuck in Cammie's booster seat. "Honey, we need to talk about this."

I rush ahead of her. "Not now." When I open the front door, Avery is sitting on the living room couch with his headphones on, typing away on his laptop. He doesn't hear me come in. Doesn't even look up from the screen.

Good. Fine.

I carry my flip-flops as I walk barefoot up the stairs to my room. *No.* Not my room. Never my room.

There's no place here that's mine. Any minute, Cammie can walk right in and there's nothing I can do to stop him. It's his room, too.

My phone buzzes in my pocket, but when I check to see who's calling, it's a number I don't recognize. Of course it's a wrong number. Who's going to call me? Not Kiersten or Gabriella. Not even Gregg would want to call me. Not after what he heard me say.

That's when it hits me. How Gregg must've felt, overhearing what I said in the bathroom. How would I feel if I heard Avery say the same thing about me?

Awful. The worst.

Oh my God. It hits me again. Slams me in the stomach. Am I Avery's Gregg?

I fling my phone across the room.

It lands on the navy-blue beanbag chair Mom bought for Cammie when he complained that all the chairs here were uncomfortable.

I grab one of the pillows from the bed, press my mouth to it, and scream. The pillow drowns out the sound. My tears make splotches that turn the pale pink flowers on the pillowcase a bright red.

There's a knock at the door.

I lift my mouth off the pillow. "In a minute, Cammie."

"It's not Cammie," Avery says.

"I'm busy."

"Maddie, come on."

"No!" I'm sure he can hear the tears in my voice. "Please. Leave me alone."

I hear his footsteps as he walks away from the door, along the hall, and down the stairs. I plant my face back on the pillow and listen to Cammie, outside playing catch with Dad, and the McLarens' next-door neighbors' dogs barking. The buzz of lawn mowers and weed cutters in the distance. Birds tweeting in the tree outside the window.

But in the bedroom, all I hear is the ticking of the little alarm clock on my nightstand, the one Grammy bought for me and Cammie for trips. Cammie grabbed it when they went down to the basement. Thought they might be down there awhile and need to know the time. This is the longest trip we've taken it on. Just down the street.

I fold myself up, my shins against the bed, head tucked into my knees. They made us do this at camp on yoga day. Child's pose. I stretch my arms out, tuck them under the pillows, and close my eyes.

He came in here. I didn't imagine it, right? Avery came in here in the middle of the night while outside it thundered and lightninged, like it was never going to stop. He sat right here, right on this bed. He said all the right things, to Cammie, to me.

Why?

Why was he so nice to me, if he was thinking about kissing Gabriella?

I stay in child's pose for the longest time. Minutes? Hours? I can't tell. The yoga teacher was right. It feels good to be all curled up like this. Tucked in. Like I'm zooming back through time to when I was a baby, safe inside my mom.

Okay, maybe not that far back. That's a little gross.

Still, there's something about being all curled up that makes me feel the tiniest bit better. Even if it fixes nothing. Even if I'm not ready to open my door and let anyone in. Even if I'm not ready to go outside into the rest of the house, where there's no way to avoid Avery and no bringing Hank back.

If I stay right here, tucked into this little ball, nothing can hurt me.

Maybe that's what Hank did when the storm came. Dogs can sense things, right? He knew the storm was coming. That's why I couldn't find him when it was time for his supper. He was trying to outrun the storm.

But he couldn't run fast enough.

He ran and ran and ran and ran. And then the tornado must have been right there. Right over him.

Did he curl into a ball, too?

Did he tuck himself up real good and remember

back to when he was a puppy? To when his mama protected him? Do dogs even think like that? Do they have memories that go that far back?

But if he was curled up all tight in a ball, how did his tag come off?

Was it when he was running? Maybe it got snagged on a branch and he kept running because he knew the tornado was coming.

That must be what happened.

I hear a little trill followed by a thump on the bed next to me. A paw presses against my outstretched arm.

Stupid cat.

That's what I think at first, but then he starts purring, like there's a motor running deep inside him. Mom said that cats only purr when they're really happy, when they feel at peace.

I untuck my head and open my eyes. And there is Louie, Peg's littlest cat, a calico, not much bigger than a kitten. Louie wouldn't have stood a chance outside in the storm. He rubs his head against my leg and looks up at me with wide green eyes and huge black pupils.

He wants me to pet him. He must.

But it feels wrong to pet him, to like him, to scratch behind his ears. That's what Hank loved. Those were the things I did for Hank.

Louie head-butts me again. Stares at me, practically begging me to reach out and touch him. *Come on,* he's thinking. *What's stopping you? Come on and pet me already. I'm so cute. How can you resist me?*

Even though only Louie is here to listen, I close my eyes and whisper, "I'll always love you, Hank. You're my favorite." And when I open my eyes, I scratch Louie right behind the ear. Just how Hank loved it. He purrs even louder and leans into my scratching.

There's another knock on the door.

"Dinner's almost ready, and Mom wants to know if you're gonna come eat with us."

"I'll be down soon," I tell Cammie, not taking my hand off Louie.

It only lasts five days. My period, that is.

Mom says I'm lucky and that I shouldn't get used to it. But I'm not counting the period days. Not really. I'm counting the days of Kiersten not texting or calling me. Of Avery barely saying a word to me except "Can you pass the butter?" or "Can you turn the volume down?" Of Gabriella not writing back to my *Can we talk?* email.

I brush my teeth in the downstairs bathroom with Cammie on Thursday night. I tell him it's because the upstairs bathroom is so crowded all the time, but really, it's because downstairs we won't run into Avery.

"Hey, Maddie?" Cammie's mouth brims with foamy toothpaste.

I spit into the sink. "Yeah?"

"Do you think Hank turned into a ghost?"

I swish some water around in my mouth and spit again. "You only turn into a ghost when you have unfinished business. Like stuff you meant to do before you died." Before this summer, I would've said I didn't believe in ghosts, but after playing with the Ouija board, I'm not so sure.

"Like saying goodbye to us?" Cammie rinses his toothbrush. "Maybe his ghost is still looking for us."

I turn off the bathroom light before we head back into the hallway.

"I don't think Hank's ghost is somewhere out there, wandering around."

"But what if he is? How do you know for sure?"

I tuck Cammie's tag into the back of his pajamas as we walk up the stairs. "If you're really worried about his ghost, we could do something special for Hank to let him know that we'll always love him."

"Like how we did that thing for Grandma?"

"The memorial? Exactly."

"Let's wait till the morning to ask Daddy. I bet he'll say yes after coffee."

Right before I go to bed, I grab my cell phone off the charger and pull up the latest text thread with Kiersten. The day after the pool party, she and her brother flew down to Florida to spend a week with her dad. I know her phone still works because she's been posting pictures pretty nonstop, just like usual. But as I scroll up, all I see are the dozens of messages I've sent her. The ones she hasn't replied to.

And it's like I'm Gregg all over again. Spamming her.

I get the message. I know what it means when she doesn't reply.

I rest my phone on the nightstand and check with Cammie, who's flipping through a Ninjago comic. "You ready to go to sleep?"

He tosses his comic to the floor, and I click off the light.

I drop another shovelful of dirt on the ground next to the small hole we dug for Hank's collar. "You want to do the last one?"

Cammie takes the shovel from me and digs out one more tiny clump of dirt. Most of it falls back into the hole.

It's been a week since Mom spotted Hank's collar on the side of the road. Mom and Dad stand behind the hole in the ground, squinting in the late-morning sun. Mom holds a small bouquet of flowers clipped from Peg's garden.

We chose a spot next to the dogwood tree in our front yard as the gravesite for Hank's collar. It's one of the few trees the tornado spared, probably because it's still so tiny.

Hank's collar jingles as I place it in the small hole in

the ground. I wonder if Cammie is thinking the same thing I am: that this is the last time we'll hear that jingle. Cammie is wearing sunglasses, so I can't see his eyes, but he's not a big crier, not anymore. He's grown up a lot this summer.

I push the dirt back over the hole, covering the collar, and pat it down with my palms. There's dirt underneath my fingernails, but I leave it there.

Mom places the flowers gently on top of the mound of dirt. She kisses her hand and presses it to the flowers. One last kiss for Hank. Even though she always talked about how dirty he was from being outside so much, she kissed his head all the time.

She reaches out her hands, one for me, one for Cammie. Dad grabs my other hand as we stand in a circle around Hank's grave.

"Maddie?" Dad asks. "Is there anything you want to say?"

I haven't planned anything for this moment, but still, I have to say something. Staring down at the flowers, I think back to the beginning. "I remember that day Mom and Dad brought you home, Hank. You were just a puppy and you were so excited about everything. You were so stoked about treats and you needed to sniff everything in the house and the yard. And you were so tiny. I didn't know how big you'd grow up to be. But you didn't change as you got older. Not really. You still needed to sniff everything and you still got so unbelievably excited about your treats." I laugh. I look up at Mom and she's laughing a little, too, even though there are tears in her eyes.

"You were a great dog, Hank. The best."

Dad squeezes my hand.

"Cammie?" Mom asks.

Cammie shakes his head.

"You were the best dog I could have asked for," Mom says. "A true wild beast, sharing our home and our hearts."

"He wasn't *that* wild," Dad says.

"Clearly, you've forgotten that time he managed to eat an entire towel," Mom says.

"Hank ate a towel?" Cammie shakes his head, like there's no way this could be true.

"When you were a baby," I say.

"Let me tell you, it's no picnic going to the emergency vet with a towel-eating dog at midnight when you're home alone with two little kids while their dad's on a business trip." Mom is smiling at Dad as she says it.

"Sorry!" Dad laughs. "I didn't exactly give Hank instructions to eat the towel while I was gone. He managed to keep his towel cravings under control when I was around."

Mom shakes her head. "Thank you, Hank. For always keeping our lives interesting."

"To Hank," Dad says, raising an imaginary glass up into the air. "For being one of a kind."

All four of us hold up our imaginary glasses. "To Hank," I say.

"To Hank."

If any of the construction workers are watching us, they're probably wondering what in the heck we're doing.

We each take a moment alone at Hank's grave to say our final goodbyes. When it's my turn, I crouch down and pat the bare dirt. I whisper, "I love you, Hank."

Mom asks if I want to take a tour of the house, now that they've put in all the exterior walls and framed the rooms, so I follow her inside. One of the construction workers gives us hard hats to wear. The hat makes my ears stick out, but Mom says I'm not allowed inside without it, so I keep it on.

There's sawdust everywhere, and it makes my nose itch. Each room we go into has at least two guys hammering away. I have to put my fingers in my ears a few times when the drilling gets too loud. We check out the new living room, which is pretty much the same size as our old living room, and the new downstairs bathroom. Pipes are sticking out, but there's still no toilet or sink. The new kitchen is bigger and will have a different layout than our old one. At least, that's what Mom says. But right now it all feels so empty without cabinets or a kitchen island. Will this really be ready in time for school?

I follow Mom up the stairs to the second floor. Our

old house had three bedrooms, but the new one has four. Mom and Dad's bedroom is over the garage this time, and twice the size, with a huge window looking out at the street. Cammie's room and the guest room are in the front of the house. Toward the back is my room and the bathroom that Cammie and I will share.

"So, what do you think of your new room?" Mom asks as the hammering quiets down.

I step through the doorway for the very first time. My old room was in the front of the house, but it makes sense for this to be my new room; it's the second-biggest bedroom after my parents'. Through the side window, I can see into Greta and the Germ's backyard.

There's a bigger window looking out into our backyard. Outside is a dry patch of grass where our old swing set was. Mom and Dad will have to get Cammie a new one.

Beyond our backyard used to be the forest. Evergreens and maples as far as you could see. The trees were so tall, though, that you couldn't see very far. But not anymore.

What I see now is the path the tornado took, how it kept going past our house and deep, deep into the forest. The trees completely flattened, all lying down in the same direction, like pickup sticks.

"It won't always look so desolate." Mom stands right behind me. "New plants and trees will grow. Nature has its way of rebuilding." She places her hand on my shoulder. "What do you think?"

I take it in. The whole room. *My* room. It's completely empty and new. A true blank slate. I can decorate it however I want. That's what Mom keeps telling me. I get to choose the paint color, the furniture, the posters. Everything. It won't feel like a little-kid room anymore, the way my old room sometimes did. Maddie's teen room, Mom calls it.

"I love it." The feeling almost takes me by surprise. "Are they going to be done with the house by the time school starts?"

"That's something Dad and I wanted to talk to you about."

"What do you mean?"

"They're working as fast as they can, and I promised Peg we'd be out of her hair by the time summer ends."

"So, where are we going?" There's this tiny lump in the back of my throat. Maybe Avery's not the only one moving. What if we have to live somewhere else when school starts?

"We're going to have a little adventure in a trailer. Right in our yard. It'll be like camping."

"We're going to live in a trailer?" Trailers are so tiny and cramped. And with all four of us? "Will I have to share a bed with Cammie?"

Mom laughs. "No, no, no. We'll have separate

sleeping areas. It'll be a tight squeeze for sure, but, Maddie, remember this: we are really, really fortunate."

"I know." I hope my face matches what I'm saying. Mom doesn't mean we're lucky that a tornado took out our house or that we get to live in a trailer. She means we're lucky we get to build a new house, right here where we've always lived. Luckier than Avery's family.

Mom's smile fades away, and her eyes crinkle at the corners. "There's something else we need to talk about, hon."

She knows. Kiersten's mom must've called to tell her what happened. Or maybe Gabby's. I swallow hard. "Oh?"

"Naomi called earlier this morning when you were in the shower." Avery's mom, not Kiersten's. "They found another place to stay. A rental that's close to where Mr. Linden works."

"They're leaving Hitchcock?"

Mom nods slowly.

Since the night Avery came home upset, I haven't heard for sure what's happening. But he and his parents left town a few days after the pool party to visit relatives. Was that when they broke the news to him?

I try to imagine a bus ride to school without Avery, but I can't. Sure, he got sick a few times and missed school, but not often. I can't picture it.

"He's leaving for real." It comes out almost a whisper. Suddenly I remember that thought I had when

Avery first mentioned moving. To invite Avery and his family to stay with us. We have the guest bedroom, and Cammie and I could share a room. But none of that matters now. It's not like there will be any extra room in a trailer.

And besides, I don't even think Avery would want to keep living with me.

I take a few steps toward the other window in my room and stare out it, toward the Germ and Greta's house. They're out on their swing set, swinging and yelling at each other. Like me and Avery used to when we were little.

Mom lingers in my room. She doesn't make me talk about it the way Dad would. She gets it. How sometimes there's nothing left to say. Sometimes it's too late for talking to make any difference.

After a few minutes, Mom clears her throat. "Dad's going to take Cammie to the movies this afternoon. You want to come to the design center with me to look at paint samples? Check out some furniture for your room? We haven't had nearly enough Mom and Maddie time this summer."

"Okay." I wonder if Mom has noticed me not talking about Kiersten this whole week. If she has, she's not saying anything.

Mom lets Dad and Cammie know about our plans as we start the walk down the street back to the McLarens' house. We pass right by Avery's. One of the blue tarps that'd been covering the gaping hole where the roof should be has blown off. It's tangled up in a tree on the edge of their yard.

I wonder if Avery and his parents even know. Or if it matters, since it looks like they're never going to live there again.

"Maddie? Come on," Mom says. "We've got a lot of work ahead of us today."

I pick up the pace and don't look back again.

26

At the design center, Mom and I pore over binders of wallpaper and strips of paint colors. There are at least a thousand different shades of white, it turns out. Not that I want white for my bedroom. White is boring. Mom agrees. She brings over this binder of light colors. Pale blues and mint greens.

I keep coming back to a page with shades of light pinky-orange, and I press my finger to a color called Desert Coral. The sample is sort of the color of Peg's cat Louie's nose, but I don't tell Mom that.

"How about this?" I ask.

Mom leans over for a closer look. "Oh, I like that one, Maddie. It has a lot of warmth to it."

Warmth? I shrug. "So, are we done?"

Mom laughs. "Well, that's one room taken care of.

What about your and Cammie's bathroom?" She lifts a heavy binder of wallpaper and plunks it down in front of me. "I was thinking of an accent wall behind the sink. Something . . . unique. Maybe a print?"

I flip through some pages. There's a crazy orange-and-green wallpaper with mushrooms and bunnies that looks like it came from the 1970s. I show that one to Mom.

She snorts, and the guy from the design center turns his head in our direction. We both giggle. "That's a little too *Alice in Wonderland* for me, thanks. But I like the idea of something with animals. Don't you think Cammie would like one with animals?"

We decide the red one with zebras is a little too crazy but then find a bird print that's perfect. Interesting enough that you want to look at it, but not so interesting that anyone who uses our upstairs bathroom will think we're crazy.

Two things done. Only about five million to go.

After finishing up at the design center, Mom brings her tote bag full of furniture catalogs and a few pads of Post-its into Fred's Pizza. We've got plenty to keep us busy while we wait for our pizza.

We grab a booth by the window, and I open up the Ikea catalog. There's a white wooden bed that looks perfect for my new room, so I press a hot-pink Post-it on that page. But then on the next page there's another bed I like, so I put a Post-it there.

I take a sip of ice water. Choosing is exhausting.

"What about this one?" Mom shows me a girlie white iron bed in the PB Teen catalog.

"Too old lady."

Mom laughs. "Don't let Peg hear you say that."

"I won't." I take another long drink of water, nearly finishing the glass.

Mom smiles and returns to flipping through her catalog, folding the corners when she finds something she likes.

After finishing with the Ikea catalog, I take a break for a moment and stare out the window. I imagine what my room will look like with the Desert Coral walls, all this new furniture, and maybe some new posters. I'm still staring out the window when a blue Volvo station wagon pulls into one of the front parking spaces and Gabriella, her mom, and her sister come out.

My mouth goes dry, and I reach for my water, but there's only ice left in the glass.

"Do you need another water?" Mom asks. "I'll try to catch the waitress when she comes back. Shouldn't be long till the pizza's ready."

I wish I were sitting on Mom's side, so my back would be to the door, but instead, I'm facing right toward the door as it opens, jingling the bell. Gabriella comes in first, followed by her sister and their mom.

I pull out another catalog from the tote bag. Even though I don't really like any of the furniture in it, I keep putting Post-it notes on all the pages. A leather chair that looks like it belongs in some lawyer's office. An ugly brass desk lamp. A magazine rack for a doctor's office. If I can just keep my head down and seem busy, maybe they won't stop by.

"Looks like you're finding lots of good stuff in that catalog."

I look up at Mom. Behind her, Geena, our waitress, walks toward us with the pizza. Pepperoni and cheese, my favorite. Except there's this lump in my throat, and another in my stomach.

"It's a hot one," Geena says. She pulls out a metal rack for the pizza to sit on. It takes up so much of the table that we have to put the catalogs away.

"Can we have a refill on the water?" Mom asks.

"Sure thing." Geena heads back to the kitchen.

I try taking a slice for myself, but the cheese is so gooey that Mom has to help, struggling with a knife and a fork to separate my slice from the rest of the pizza. While Mom's grabbing her slice, I glance at the table where Gabriella is sitting. Her mom and sister are laughing about something, but Gabriella is staring down at her phone.

I wonder if she even saw me.

"What are you waiting for?" Mom asks.

"It's too hot still." I blow on my slice.

"Like that's stopped you in the past," she teases, biting into the tip of her slice. Mom always chews with her mouth closed, like me, not like Cammie and Dad, who basically eat like animals. And Hank, he ate like an animal, too. Though, to be fair, he was an animal. I pick at my crust.

The waitress comes by with a pitcher of ice water to refill our glasses. "Anything else I can get you?"

Mom's mouth is full of pizza, so I answer, "No, thank you. We're all set."

Geena heads over to Gabriella's table next. I try not to look, not to keep checking, but I can't help myself.

Mom looks in that direction, too. "Is that Gabriella? We must've missed them come in. Go on over and say hi, honey."

"But the waitress is there now."

I take the smallest bite of my pizza and start chewing. I saw this article online once when I was supposed to be doing homework about how, ideally, you should be chewing each bite twenty-five times. No way do I ever chew something twenty-five times, but right now I try. One, two, three, four.

The waitress has left their table. I could go over now and talk to Gabriella. I should.

Fifteen, sixteen, seventeen.

"Mads, what's going on?" Mom asks.

I point to the food in my mouth.

"You've been chewing that bite for so long it's probably disintegrated." She looks me right in the eye. The edges of her eyes crinkle. "Maddie?"

I glance over at Gabriella. She's wearing a new purple headband. She must have replaced the one I stole from her. *Stole from her.*

I'd never stolen anything before. Not even when the Dippin' Dots cart was left unattended at Six Flags and pretty much our entire fifth-grade class helped themselves to some dots. Not even then.

But I did it to Gabriella. Took what was hers.

As if that would even out what she'd done to me.

"I don't want to talk about it," I say quietly.

The pizza slice goes limp in my hand when I pick it up. I take another bite. This time I only chew a few times before I swallow.

"Maddie, you know I can't accept that as an answer. Come to think of it, you haven't had much to say about Kiersten and Gabriella for the past week." Mom sighs and rubs her forehead. "You know you can come to me if you need to talk about something."

Another bite.

No, I think. *I can't. You wouldn't understand. You would never let a boy get between you and your friends. You don't believe in that. Men, boys, guys—whatever. They're not worth it. You wouldn't understand what it felt like to see Gabriella with Avery. To know she kissed him. Like being slammed in the stomach. Like seeing that your house is gone, gone, gone.*

That idea that I'd held in my head for so long, of me and Avery, was gone, gone, gone. In an instant.

But it's more than that. It's all gone. Kiersten keeping secrets from me, secretly planning matching outfits with Gabby, going on trips with Gabby's family. My best friend was going, going, gone, too.

Another bite.

Mom is still looking at me, waiting for me to say something. I keep chewing.

"Okay," she says, lowering her voice. "Fine. Not in here. I get that. But once we're in the car, I need you to fill me in. I can't help you if you won't tell me what's going on."

I finish chewing that bite and pause before I take another. "Okay."

We're quiet for the rest of the meal. Once Mom has paid, we head back out to the car. As we walk past Gabby's table, she acts like she doesn't see me either.

Mom puts the leftovers in the trunk while I climb into the front seat. When Mom gets in, she hesitates before turning the key in the ignition.

"Can you please tell me what's going on, honey?"

The car is stifling after sitting out in the sun with no air-conditioning for the past forty-five minutes. "Can we turn on the AC first?"

The car thrums to life and hot air shoots out of the

229

vents. Mom backs the car out of the parking spot. "The car will cool off in a little bit, but in the meantime, I'm listening."

"So, at the pool party," I start to say. But that's not right. "Actually, it was at the dance. . . ." The words get caught in my throat. The thing is, I don't know how to talk to Mom about this. A bad grade on a test, a stupid fight with Kiersten? Sure. It's easy to talk to Mom about those things. But boys? *Avery?* We've never talked about boys before. It's different with Kiersten and her mom.

"What happened at the dance?" Mom waits for an opening in traffic to pull out of the parking lot.

"Avery," I finally say. "He asked Gabriella to dance."

"Okay."

I go back to the beginning and tell her how Kiersten said he wanted to dance with me, and how he didn't and so I had to ask Gregg to dance with me, and how it was the most awkward four minutes of my entire life. But then how nice Avery was on the way back from the dance. How could he be so nice after he'd just rejected me? I tell her everything that happened. Well, except for one thing. I don't tell her how Avery came into my room that night during the storm. That one thing I keep secret. That one thing I want all for myself still.

Mom puts the blinker on to turn up our street. On both sides of the street, I can still see the chopped-off half trees. It feels like the tornado is never going to go away. Like it's always going to be here, reminding me that nothing good can last.

I tell her about the pool party, and how my best friend lied to me. How she never told me she knew Gabriella had kissed Avery. Why would she keep that a secret? How could she not know how awful I'd feel when I finally heard?

As we head up our hill, Mom's fingers lightly tap on the steering wheel. I wonder what she's thinking. It can't be any worse than what I've already thought about myself for the last week.

"Why aren't you saying anything?" I ask.

"When we decided to all stay at the McLarens' with the Lindens . . . we never thought—I mean, you're only going into seventh grade. I knew we were getting close to the boy-crazy years, I just didn't think they were already upon us. We left you and Avery unattended and . . ."

"Mom!"

"What, Maddie? There are real concerns here."

"Did you listen to me? At all?" I can't believe I have to explain it to my own mom. That she has completely missed the point. "Mom, he doesn't like me! *Nothing* was going to happen. He likes Gabriella. Not me!"

Mom pulls the car into the McLarens' driveway, cuts the engine, and rolls down the windows. She takes a deep breath. "I have been listening, Maddie. Sweetie, calm down."

I unbuckle my seat belt. "No," I say, opening my car door. The smell of the pizza in the trunk makes me want to gag. "You're not listening at all. Not really. I knew I couldn't talk to you about this."

I slam the car door behind me.

27

When I get to my room, Cammie is in there, Legos spread out all over the floor and on both of our beds.

"Cammie, can you go downstairs?"

"I'm busy." He bends the leg of his Lego spider contraption.

I raise my voice. "I don't care if you're busy. I'm older than you and I get to make the rules for our room and you need to go downstairs now." I grab the Lego spider out of his hands. "Now!"

"Okay, okay."

I hand him back the spider as he gets up and shut the door behind him. I brush the Legos aside, lie down on my bed, and close my eyes. There's no one else in here this time except for me. No cats. No little brother. No friends, not that I even think I have any. No parents. No Hank. Not even the ghost of Hank. Just me.

Why did I think Mom would be able to help?

She doesn't get it. She can't remember how it feels to like someone and not have him like you back. And worse, to have the person that they do like be someone you know. Someone you have to see all the time, too. Whether you want to or not. Someone who's going to weasel her way in between you and your best friend.

Mom can't help me with this, at least not the same way she could help fix things that went wrong when I was little.

I grab my phone and start scanning through the pictures. Journeying back in time. Me and Kiersten and Gabby at the sleepover. The three of us getting fro-yo at the mall. Dressed up at the dance, before the tornado, before everything changed. The first time Gabby hung out with us at Kiersten's house, that day we made burritos and Kiersten's exploded all over her white T-shirt.

And back further. Me and Kiersten having the biggest snowball fight ever. Me and Kiersten at the Hitchcock Christmas-tree lighting. Me and Kiersten rocking Spirit Day in the fall.

Me, and Kiersten.

I listen to my breath. The in and out, in and out. The ticking of the clock.

And then I hear something else, a sound from the

other side of the wall. A thump and then wheels rolling. Avery and his parents must've just gotten back.

You can't build a house in a day. That's what Dad explained to Cammie. *But you can with a Lego house,* Cammie had said. And of course, he was right.

You can't build a real *house in a day,* Dad went on to say. And he explained how you need to start from the ground up. How, without a solid foundation, the whole thing can crumble so easily. A real house has to be sturdy and well built to weather the storms.

You start with a foundation.

I walk over to the mirror and stare back at myself. Cammie isn't the only one who grew up this summer. I did, too. I'm taller. The shorts I got from Kiersten at the beginning of the summer are shorter on me now. Even shorter if I cuff them. I roll them up and look back in the mirror. *Better.* I fix my ponytail. Stare into the mirror again. Maybe by next summer, I'll fill out the top of my bathing suit. I take another deep breath. *Okay. It's time to start again.*

I knock on Avery's door.

"Yeah?"

"It's Maddie. Can I come in?"

"Sure."

I open the door myself.

His normally super-organized room is in total disarray. Clothes in messy piles all over the bed. Suitcases opened up on the floor. He's sitting at his desk with one of the summer-reading books I still haven't looked at. Only Avery would still read the summer-reading books for a school he's not going to.

"You're packing already?"

Avery nods.

"When are you moving?"

"Not until Friday, but my mom keeps nagging me to start packing, so I figured I should."

"Where are you moving to?"

"Palmer."

"Oh, that's not *that* far away."

"It's close to work for my dad. My parents are renting an apartment by the school so I can walk, which . . . I guess is nice? I don't know. It seems weird not to be taking a bus."

And not to be going to our school. But I don't say that part aloud. I don't want to rub it in.

"At least, you won't have to listen to Mrs. Walter's crazy seventies music every morning." Our bus driver has the worst taste in music.

Avery laughs. "That's true. I hadn't thought of that."

We're both quiet for a moment.

"I don't think I had the chance to tell you how sorry I am about Hank. I was really hoping I'd—I mean that he'd come back. There's all those stories on the news about pets that get separated from their owners and then reunited after tons of time has passed."

"That would've been really cool," I say. But the grown-up part of me doesn't believe in those fairy tales anymore. Avery places his book on the desk.

"Can I ask you something?" I say.

"Yeah."

"Why didn't you ever tell me . . . about you and Gabriella? I mean, you didn't even mention it, and she didn't, and . . ."

Avery chews on his thumb for a second. "I don't know. I guess . . ."

"What?" I ask quietly.

"I didn't think it mattered to you."

"Why?"

"Well, don't you like Gregg?"

I clap my hand over my mouth to stop myself from laughing. "What?"

"Not that you heard this from me, but Gregg likes you, and you were the one who asked him to dance."

"But that was only because—"

"Because what?"

"N-n-nothing," I stammer. "Because he was there and I needed to dance with someone. Because everyone was dancing with someone."

"It was so weird, right? I didn't think they were going to play any slow songs, and then they did and I—I panicked."

So choosing to dance with Gabriella was *panicking*? Then what was kissing her? I wonder.

"Anyway, it's not like she's my girlfriend or anything. Can we talk about something else now? Anything?"

"Um, okay." Everything Avery just said has created about five thousand more questions in my head, but they're ones better discussed with Kiersten, once we're talking again. "How are the Red Sox doing?" It's the first thing that pops into my head.

"Let me check." Avery grabs his laptop, and I pull up another chair to sit next to him. He opens up the web browser, but it doesn't fill the entire screen. There are a few documents on the side that I can see. Most look like school assignments, except for one of them. The one called "Hank."

I point to it. "What's that?"

"Oh, um." Avery seems flustered. "This is probably going to seem a little weird."

Weirder than how I've been acting toward him all summer? I doubt it.

He clicks to open the document. It's a spreadsheet of all the addresses in our neighborhood, with *X*'s next to some and notes next to others.

"What is this?"

"I was trying to be scientific," Avery says. "About finding Hank."

"You were trying to find Hank? Wait—how? And when?"

"It's pretty simple, actually," he says. "I pulled up our neighborhood on Google Maps and started with a one-mile radius from your house. And I put all those houses on the spreadsheet and called them to ask if they had seen Hank or found anything from him. And then, when I finished that, I added the next mile out."

"You called them? All these people?"

There are dozens of addresses on this list, most of them marked with the date Avery spoke to someone. It's all organized and scientific. Just like Avery.

"I biked to some of them. But yeah."

"How come you never said anything about it?"

He shrugs. "I didn't want you to be more sad than you already were. What if it seemed like there was a lead and then it turned out to be a dead end? Or what if someone found him and he was . . ." He can't even say the word.

"I was pretty sad when my mom found his collar," I say. "I don't know how it came off. It never came off before. But it must've snagged on a tree or something."

"Where did she find it?"

"At the top of the hill. By the Lewises' old house."

Avery scrolls down the spreadsheet. "Did she stop in and talk to anyone there?"

"I don't think so. She just picked it up and drove over to get me from the pool."

Avery clicks on the entry for the Lewises' address on the spreadsheet. In the notes field are all these dates and phrases: *left voice mail, out of service, voice mail not set up yet, try again?*

"You never talked to anyone there?"

Avery shakes his head. "Your mom really found the collar by the Lewises' old house?"

"Yeah. Cammie was in the car with her."

"Do you want to bike over there tomorrow morning?"

Does he think I could say anything besides yes?

"Of course I do."

My heart is beating so loudly I wonder if Avery can hear it. He closes the spreadsheet. I can hear every breath coming out of his nose.

I can't believe he did this for me. On top of everything else he was dealing with—losing his house, having to move—he'd spent his free time on this. *For me.*

That's what you do for a friend, though. Anything. Everything. Avery being so nice to me even though he was kissing Gabriella, it wasn't to be mean. Or to lead me on. It was because he was—*is*—my friend. A good friend.

And that's when I realize what I need to do. How to fix things with Kiersten, with Gabriella. The foundation was cracked. My jealousy ruined it. But now I know what I need to do to rebuild. Or at least try to.

If I don't leave Avery's room real fast, I'm going to start to cry.

"I think I hear my mom calling," I say. "I should probably go see what she wants."

"Sure." Avery turns off the sound as Red Sox highlights start to play. "What time do you want to go tomorrow?"

"Knock on my door when you're awake," I say, standing in his doorway. "I'll be ready."

As Avery and I wait on the steps at the Lewises' old house, we hear noises from inside. The sounds of a baby—or babies—crying and a TV blaring. I hope they can hear us knocking.

I'd ring the doorbell, but there's a small sign written in marker taped right above it: *Baby sleeping. You wake him, he's yours.* Neither Avery nor I want a baby right now.

Last night, I could hardly sleep, I was so excited at the idea of seeing Hank again. But when I woke up this morning, I remembered that kind of thing happens only in fairy tales or the movies. Could I really be lucky enough to find Hank this way?

"Should we knock again?" I ask.

Avery leans his ear against the door. "I'm not sure they can even hear the doorbell in there anyway."

I chew on my lip. We're *this* close. They've got to answer the door.

"What if we try calling them again?"

Avery pulls out his cell phone. "I think I still have their number in here." He holds the phone to his ear. "It's ringing."

I cross my fingers.

"Hello? Hi, uh, I'm at your front door right now. I knocked a few times, but nobody answered and—"

Just then the door opens. Standing in the doorframe is a guy with messy blond hair. He has a crying baby in one arm and another little guy clinging to his leg.

"Sorry about that," he says. "This place can be kind of a zoo sometimes." He laughs. "On our good days. How can I help you kids? You selling something for school?"

I clear my throat. "Actually, no. Not today. It's about my dog, Hank. He went missing during the tornado, and my mom found his collar on the side of the road by your house. We were wondering if maybe you'd seen him."

"Your dog, huh?" He scratches at his head and passes the baby off to his wife, who waves at us before heading up the stairs. "You're from the neighborhood?"

"We live further down Hollow Road," I say. "I'm Maddie Evans."

"And I'm Avery." He reaches out his hand.

"Nice to meet you two. I'm Isaac, and my little guy, that's Cooper. We just moved in here a few weeks ago. Came out from Illinois—you know, where the tornadoes are supposed to happen. I still can't believe one crossed this street! That's just—it's crazy."

"Yeah," Avery says. "Pretty unbelievable."

"So, back to your dog . . . you say he went missing during the storm?"

I tell him about how I was supposed to feed Hank his supper but couldn't find him. And how Mom and Dad didn't see him again after that. How it was like he vanished, except, well, he couldn't. He was a real dog. His body had to go somewhere.

"Now, I don't want to get your hopes up, not just yet. But when Emma, my wife, and I moved in here, she was sneezing up a storm. We don't have any pets—trust me, the kids are enough—and she's always been allergic to dogs. But the weird thing is, the folks we bought the house from, they said not a problem, their tenants weren't allowed to have pets. You know, so we took them at face value—we bought this place sight unseen."

"So, you think they did have a dog?" Avery asks.

"Well, based on how sick Emma was when we moved in here . . . it seems awfully likely." He reaches in his pocket and pulls out his phone. "You know, I have their number from when we were trying to coordinate utility switchovers. Let me give them a ring. You guys want to come in for a minute?"

I glance over at Avery, who nods. "Sure."

We find our way over to the couch, pushing a few board books out of the way. From upstairs, we can hear Emma singing a song to the baby. Cooper finally lets go of his dad's leg and plays with a puzzle on the floor.

Isaac turns down the TV and paces with the phone to his ear. "Hey, yeah, sorry to bother you. I've got this kid here from down the street. Said she lost her dog around the time of the tornado. You folks didn't happen to— Whoa, no way! Okay. Yeah. Uh-huh." Isaac flashes me a thumbs-up.

I grab Avery's shoulder, not even thinking. "Oh my God! They have him!"

Isaac gestures for me to get on the phone, and I leap off the couch. My foot crunches on some stray Cheerios, and I grab the phone from him.

"Hello?" My voice shakes, but in the best way possible.

A woman's voice is on the other end. "I'm so sorry— his fur was all matted and he didn't have a tag. I thought for sure he was a stray. We were a few days away from moving to Springfield and everything was all mixed up. We thought we were rescuing him."

"But he's okay? He's not hurt? Are you sure it's him?"

"Your dog's a sweetheart, honey. Just as sweet as can be."

"His name's Hank," I say.

"Hey, Hank!" she shouts, and then lowers her voice back to a normal volume. "You should've seen the look on his face when I called him that. He never did like being called Oliver."

I laugh and wipe a tear off my cheek. I don't even care if Avery sees me crying.

"Now for the important question: When do you think you and your mom or dad can come by to pick him up? Hank sure looks like he's ready to go home."

Mom insists that Avery join us for the drive out to Springfield later that afternoon, since he's the reason we're getting Hank back in the first place.

Cammie sits in his booster seat in between me and Avery. "I knew he was still out there somewhere," he says. "I just knew it."

"How did you know?" Avery asks.

"Because I never saw his ghost." Cammie keeps kicking his leg against the cup holders. "If Hank was really dead, his ghost would have slept on my bed every night."

"Makes sense," Avery says.

The drive to Springfield feels like it takes ten hours, even though it's more like half an hour. Mom can't settle on a radio station and Cammie has a billion questions about everything today: if Hank will still remember us (of course), who are the slowest and fastest base runners for the Red Sox, where boogers come from, etc. His mind doesn't want to quiet down. At least Avery is willing to treat his questions like real questions.

The whole way there, I keep thinking about what must have gone through Hank's mind the day of the tornado. He'd run home, right? To his very first home.

Maybe he knew his house—where he lived with us—was in peril. Maybe he could feel it. Animals can sense things like that, right?

And so he ran and ran. All the way back to the first place he'd ever called home. Except the right people weren't there. It's been years since the Lewises lived there. And his mama—his dog mama—she wasn't there anymore either.

Did he feel like he didn't have a home? Did he give up then?

And how did he lose his collar? Will we ever know what truly happened that day?

Mom exits the highway and takes us into a busy neighborhood. The houses are smooshed right on top of each other and there are hardly any trees. Just little patches of grass in front of all the houses. Not nearly as much yard as Hank was used to.

"What if they change their mind and don't give him back?" Cammie asks as Mom parallel-parks in front of a small white house.

"That's not going to happen. I talked to them on the phone, remember?"

Before we're even out of the car, the front door of the house opens. Out comes a little girl, not much older than Cammie, with frizzy blond hair and a Popsicle stain on her white tank top.

And behind her is Hank.

A bit of slobber drips from his mouth, in which he's got not one, not two, but three tennis balls. Not exactly a record for Hank, but still.

"It's him! It's him!" Cammie shouts, fumbling with the seat belt. I leave Avery to help with that. I can't wait one second longer.

"Hank!" He barrels straight toward me as I step out of the car and into the humid air. Jumps up on me, even though we trained him not to. One of the tennis balls falls out. "Hey, buddy." There are so many spots I haven't petted in so long that I don't know where to start, so I attack him all over. Scratch and pet behind his ears and all over his back. Once he settles down, I hug him close to my chest and press my cheek against his.

"Oh my gosh!" Cammie proceeds to maul Hank, getting him all riled up again.

"Watch out," Mom says. "Don't give him too much attention. He might come to demand it every day once we're home."

Avery squeezes in for a pet.

"I can't believe you found him," I say. "We owe you a reward or something."

"You don't owe me anything," he says. "Okay, maybe an ice cream."

"He loves when you scratch behind his ears," the little girl says, sitting over on the concrete steps leading up to her house. Her name is Caroline.

When I get closer, I can hear her sniffle. Even though she's trying to be brave, it must be hard for her. For almost two months, Hank's been her dog. She's taken care of him, given him food and water and love. But tonight, the end of her bed will be empty.

"You know, you can always come visit him if you want to. We're not that far away." I glance back at Mom, hoping she'll jump in.

"Of course," Mom says. "Though it sounds like you're getting a new puppy, right?"

Caroline sniffles again and smiles. "We're getting a new puppy next week."

"What kind?" Avery asks.

"A labradoodle."

The construction guy. Mom and Dad must have hooked them up.

"Thanks for taking such good care of Hank," I say.

"He's a great dog."

Caroline's mom butts in. "He sure is." She reaches down to give Hank another pat. "I'm sorry to hear about what happened to your house. Losing your home and your pet all at once? That must've been hard on you folks."

"They've been real troupers," Mom says, giving my shoulder a squeeze.

I wrap my arms around Hank and press my cheek against his golden-brown fur again. He smells like he's ready for a good bath. I wonder what he's going to think when he meets all of Peg's cats.

"You ready to go home, buddy?"

When we get back to the McLarens' house, I wait for the right moment, when Cammie is downstairs playing Go Fish with Mom, and head up to our room, closing the door behind me.

"Here goes nothing," I say to Louie, who hops up to cuddle next to me. Turns out he's not the kind of cat that will sit on your lap—he doesn't even sit on Peg's lap and Peg feeds him—but he sure loves sitting next to you.

I dial Kiersten's number and listen to the rings.

One.

She's not going to answer.

Two.

Sure, she's back from Florida. But that doesn't mean things will go back to normal.

Three.

She's probably over at Gabriella's house.

Four.

They're probably making plans for how they're going to conquer junior high without me.

Five—

"Hey."

It's been so long I almost don't recognize her voice.

She clears her throat. "Sorry, I think I'm choking on a piece of popcorn." (Maybe you can't actually forget someone's voice in one week.) I hear her cough a few times. "Okay, I think it's gone. What's up?"

What's up?

"I get why you didn't reply to my texts or send me any pictures while you were down in Florida. I do. I wasn't being a good friend, and—"

"My phone died."

"Wait—really?"

"Yeah. I accidentally dropped it in the pool at my dad's condo, and I only got a new one today."

"Oh. So, you weren't—"

"Maddie."

"What?"

"Even if that hadn't happened . . . I was still upset. Everything that happened at the pool party. You and Gabriella fighting? I hated that."

"Me too," I say. "I'm sorry. I wish I hadn't said those things. But still, I just . . . I can't believe you knew that whole time and didn't say anything."

"I know." Kiersten gets quiet on the other side. "I'm sorry about that—I am. But what was I supposed to do? You told me not to say a word to Gabby about the emails from Gregg. And I kept that promise. When Gabby made me pinkie-swear I wouldn't tell a soul that she kissed Avery, what was I supposed to do then? I don't like lying. Or, you know, not saying anything. But I didn't feel like I had a choice. It's no fun being stuck in the middle, trust me."

I had never seen it that way.

"Well, it's no fun being left behind either."

"What are you talking about?" Kiersten asks.

"When you went on vacation with Gabby and her family. I mean, I get that she could only bring one person, I do . . . but"—I suck in a deep breath—"I don't want to lose you, too."

"Lose me?"

"That's what it feels like. At least a little. Losing my house. And Hank. Avery rejecting me at the dance. Losing you to Gabby."

"Maddie, how are you losing me?"

Louie rolls over onto his back and I stroke his tummy.

"Gabby's really fun and nice. Of course you're going to want to be friends with her. I mean, obviously Avery thought she was cooler than me. I thought maybe you'd decide the same thing."

"Maddie."

"What?"

"I like hanging out with Gabby because she's actually really fun and smart and a good listener. And because she lives right next door. Do you know how long I've been waiting for someone my age to move into my neighborhood? You've always had Avery. I haven't had anybody."

"You're right." I chew on my lip, still not entirely sure I believe her.

"Hey, can I tell you something?"

"Yeah." *Always.*

"There's this cute boy, Nate, that lives next door to my dad's place in Florida."

"No way. What's he like? Did you talk to him?"

"Tan and sort of tall, but with really blue eyes, and thick eyelashes, but the kind that still look good on a boy, you know? I talked to him a couple of times by the pool. Bryant was being all obnoxious about it. I don't know how he could tell I had a crush on him! I was playing it *so cool,* Maddie. Like, you'd barely believe it was me. My hands didn't sweat or anything when I talked to him."

So unfair. I wish my hands would stop sweating around Avery. "How did you stay so chill? I need tips!"

Kiersten laughs. "Maybe . . . maybe it was because I knew I might never see him again. Like, what was the worst thing that could happen if I embarrassed myself? I was heading back to Massachusetts in a couple of days anyway."

"Good point. Maybe that's what I need to do next time. Pretend there's a good chance I'll never see Avery again. Better than watching YouTube videos."

"Watching YouTube videos?"

"Before the pool party, I watched all these YouTube videos on flirting. That's how I ended up with the cheese curls in my hair! Turns out you *cannot* learn everything on YouTube."

"Oh, Mads." Kiersten's voice softens.

"What?"

"You don't need to watch videos to learn how to flirt."

"Clearly! I need a whole class or something."

Kiersten laughs. "No, that's not what I mean. The right boy's going to like the real you. Even if you have cheese curls in your hair."

"The real me. Yikes."

"I'm serious," Kiersten says. "You don't have to be perfect."

I don't have to be perfect. It takes hearing my best friend say that, over the phone after not hearing her voice for a whole week, for it to sink in. Why did I think I had to be? Where'd that idea even come from anyway?

Gabby probably isn't perfect. She just seems that way because I don't know her well enough yet. I'm sure she has flaws. Just like Kiersten's a little bit bossy sometimes and Avery chews on his thumbs.

Maybe that's the foundation—the first layer—to

friendship. The kind that gets you through junior high and everything else that comes after. Knowing you don't have to be perfect, and that nobody else is either. Even Avery.

"Maddie?"

"Sorry," I say. "I was just thinking about something."

"Someone named Avery?"

"Maybe a little."

"Is he really leaving?" Kiersten asks.

"Yeah," I say. I hear the thuds of heavier feet coming down the hallway. "Uh-oh." Louie's ears perk up and he rights himself. "Better hide."

"Hide? From what?" Kiersten asks.

"Sorry, I was talking to the cat."

Hank nudges his head in the door. Louie backs up on the bed as Hank trots over to say hi. Right before he gets there, Louie bounds across the bed and shoots out of the room. "Sorry, Hank."

"Wait, *Hank's* there?"

"Oh my gosh, I didn't tell you yet!" Hank jumps up on the end of my bed, and while I tell my best friend everything that happened, I run my fingers through his fur. It's just like it used to be. Or maybe it's better. I scratch and scratch around his ears. Definitely better.

31

With the start of school just a couple of weeks away now, Mom and Dad and I are super busy getting everything ready. The trailer is being delivered in about a week, and there's so much to do for the house still. You'd think these construction workers would know what they're doing, but evidently not all the time. They forgot to put electrical outlets in my bedroom! How am I supposed to charge up my phone? Sheesh.

Mom and I have made about a thousand trips to Target because it turns out there are so many things you need for junior high. Thirty-seven, to be exact. My new science teacher even told us which binder to buy—not three inches, not one inch, it has to be two inches. And it's hard to find a two-inch binder that's blue, my favorite color. But it must be done.

I'm lying out on a blanket in the McLarens' backyard with Hank on Friday afternoon after camp, still feeling like my head is going to explode any minute, when Kiersten calls.

"I'm going to die." From the tone of her voice, it doesn't sound like she means for real.

"What?"

"The bus schedule! Did you see it?"

I shift over on the blanket so I'm out of the sun. "Not yet. What's it say?"

"My bus comes at six-fifty-five. That's before seven! How am I going to wake up that early? I'll be late every day."

"When does my bus come?"

"Hold on. Checking. Checking."

Hank rests his head on his paws.

"What does it say?"

"Your bus route won't load. Probably because Bryant's hogging all the Wi-Fi watching Netflix!" She raises her voice for that last bit.

"I'll see if anyone's on the computer here and check it," I say. "Later!"

I head in through the back door and notice a bunch of suitcases and bags piled up in the foyer. Avery comes down the stairs with a black duffel bag.

"You guys are leaving?" I ask, even though I know the answer.

"Yup," Avery says. "My dad just picked up keys for the apartment." He adds the duffel bag to the pile.

"That's so exciting," I say. My voice catches on that last word. This is it. My final moments sharing a house with Avery. "Can I help you carry some stuff down?"

"There's only a few things left," he says. "I've got it."

"I don't mind." I follow him up the stairs.

His room is back to looking like it belongs to Peg and Frank. The bed is stripped of the sheets. The desk is free of his laptop and all its cords. All that's left is one more small suitcase and, over in the corner of the room in a sunbeam, the guitar.

It must've sat there all summer. Neither of us ever played it. I pick it up and wipe my finger along the top. Dust flies in every direction.

"We never learned how to play," I say.

"Guess we were busy with other things."

I take a few stabs at strumming. It sounds terrible, like I belong in a band with Cammie and that xylophone he played with as a baby.

Avery laughs. "You're a natural."

"Naturally bad."

"You should take lessons. Who knows, maybe you're the next Taylor Swift."

I stifle a snort. "Yeah, right."

We carry the last few things to the front door. I rest the guitar on top of the bags.

"That's everything," he says. "My parents should be back soon." He turns on the TV and is just sitting down on the couch when he jumps up. "Almost everything!" He dashes up the stairs.

There's scratching and moaning at the sliding glass door in the kitchen. Hank!

"Sorry, buddy. I didn't forget about you, I swear." I freshen up his bowl with cold water and set it down on the floor.

"Almost forgot this." Avery walks into the kitchen holding his toothbrush. He digs through the drawer looking for a ziplock bag.

"Hey, Avery?"

He pops his head up when he finds one. "Yeah?"

"I hope that everything works out, you know, with your house."

He shrugs. "There's not much I can do about it."

"I know," I say. "It's weird. The whole time we've been here, I couldn't wait to get home and have my own room again. But I think I'm going to miss it a little." Miss *him*. That's what I mean to say. But I can't get the words out.

"Me too."

He heads back into the living room to watch TV

while he waits for his parents to return. I join him. The bus schedule isn't going anywhere. But this is my last time with Avery.

A week after Avery and his parents leave, our trailer gets delivered. I didn't think it would be sitting smack in the middle of our front yard for everyone to see, but Dad says we have no choice in the matter—and to remember it's temporary.

I'm not sure he understands that some of the kids are probably going to make fun of me on the bus for it. But I try to push that thought away because, well, what other choice do I have.

It's pretty easy to push almost all my thoughts away, sharing a tiny trailer with Cammie, because I can never hear myself think. I got so used to how big the McLarens' house was and the fact that I only had to share a room with my brother.

Mom wasn't exactly lying when she said that Cammie and I wouldn't be sharing a *bed*. What she didn't say was that we would be sharing bunk beds . . . in a closet!

The entire trailer is about the size of the room Cammie and I shared at the McLarens' house. And the living room and the kitchen are basically the same room.

At least, Hank gets to sleep outside in the new doghouse Dad bought for him. I went with him to pick it out and asked if I could have one, too.

Dad didn't laugh, which was fine because it wasn't a joke. I was serious. Some of those doghouses were big enough for a sleeping bag.

It's temporary.

It's an adventure.

You're lucky.

I have to use those phrases like a mantra when Cammie's playing with ninja turtles right below me as I'm scrambling to finish the last summer-reading assignment, *Johnny Tremain,* on Friday night. The first day of school is Tuesday. Dad says I can't play the "tornado card" and that he can't believe I waited *all summer* to do my summer reading.

Sorry, Dad. I was a little distracted.

"Blam! Blam blam! You're dead, suckaaaah."

"Cammie! Language!" Mom shouts from the couch.

"Can't the turtles all get along?" Dad asks from over by the stove. He's making a stir-fry, so the whole trailer smells like onions and spices. The pan sizzles and crackles. Dad was right when he said it would be like camping. We're always going to smell like our food and how it was cooked.

"Nope!" Cammie replies.

Plastic smashes plastic below me, and I pop in my earbuds.

I've got to finish the last thirty pages of *Johnny Tremain* before Kiersten's mom picks me up for the carnival, and I only have an hour.

It's temporary.

It's temporary.

It's temporary.

32

"We'll meet up back at this gate—gate A—at nine o'clock. That's nine o'clock sharp, girls. None of this nine-fifteen business, all right?" Kiersten's mom looks each of us in the eye. Kiersten, me, Gabriella. She's trying to be tough, but she isn't fooling me.

"Yup, yup." I stare at the Ferris wheel, arcing above all the games where the carnies basically take your money as you try but fail to win the big stuffed panda. The carnival is a kaleidoscope of bright colors and flashing lights.

"All right, then. Have fun, girls. Nine o'clock!"

"Yeah, yeah, Mom." Kiersten grins, turning to me and Gabriella. "Where should we go first?"

We head down the first row, scoping out the food choices: cotton candy, candy apples, deep-fried Oreos, ice cream sundaes, fried dough, pizza. I should have eaten less of Dad's stir-fry to leave more room for all this stuff.

"Candy apples?" Kiersten heads straight toward them.

Gabriella shakes her head. "I can't," she says. And then she smiles wide, showing off the new silver wires on her teeth.

"When did this happen?" Kiersten asks.

Gabriella sighs. "I really thought if I prayed hard enough, my teeth would end up straight and I wouldn't have to get them. I've known it was coming all summer."

"You prayed for no braces?" Kiersten laughs. "Sorry, I know it's not funny."

"How long will you have them for?" I ask.

"The orthodontist said something like two years." Gabriella pouts.

"Well, I think you can still have cotton candy." I point to the booth. "My treat."

"You don't have to," Gabriella says. Maybe she thinks I'm trying to buy her off—trying to make up for what I said at the pool party by getting her a cotton candy.

"No," I say to her. "I do."

This is the first time I've seen her since that day. She's been on some text threads with Kiersten and me, but it's not the same. I know I need to talk to her alone, and I've been thinking of what to say—trying out some of my apologies on Hank—but I need to find the right moment.

I step up to the counter. "Three cotton candies, please." I hand over six dollars. We each choose our colors; Kiersten takes pink, and Gabby and I go for blue.

We walk through the arcade, pulling apart the sticky treat. Up ahead is a lady with a crystal ball, telling fortunes. Kiersten spots her. "You guys want to do fortunes?"

"I think I'll pass," I say, "but you should."

"Sorry, K. I'm with Maddie."

Kiersten hands the fortune-teller her cash while Gabby and I wait across the way, watching as a little boy and his dad try to win a goldfish by tossing a Ping-Pong ball in the right fishbowl.

I reach my hand into my pocket and feel for the purple headband. I take a deep breath. "Hey, Gabby?"

"Uh-huh."

"Remember when we played the Ouija board at your house earlier this summer?"

Gabriella nods. Her lips and tongue are all blue. Mine must be, too.

"I was still mad about you and Avery at the dance—well, I guess that's probably obvious now. Anyway, when I went to the bathroom, I took something. It was stupid and I never should have done it. I never should have kept it this long either." I pull the headband out of my pocket.

Gabriella takes it from my hand. "I did kind of wonder where this went." She wraps it around her wrist like a bracelet.

"You were right, you know? What you said at the pool party. I was being selfish about Avery."

Gabby nods. "Well, I probably could have found a nicer way to say it."

"I tried to think of what it was like from where you were standing, you know? I've never been the new kid at school. I've lived in Hitchcock—this tiny town—my whole life, but when school starts, we'll all be new kids. Trying to figure everything out all over again."

The little boy holds up his goldfish in the plastic bag, like it's the coolest thing in the entire world, not some goldfish you could get at the pet store for fifty cents. It feels like forever ago, being that little.

"I guess what I'm trying to say is that I get why you said yes to Avery when he asked you to dance. And kiss! Bah! I mean, who would say no to that?"

Gabby laughs. "He didn't *ask* me."

"He didn't? Did you ask him?"

Gabby shakes her head, laughing even harder. "Nooo! Maddie."

"What?" I'm surprised by how much I want to know

how it happened. Gabby's the only friend I have who's kissed someone. I need to file this away for later.

"It's the kind of thing that happens really fast, you know?"

I nod, like maybe then she'll think I do know. "How did it happen?"

She lowers her voice. "We were waiting at the back of the line to go up the slide at Gregg's pool. We were just talking, and . . . I don't know—it felt like it was the right time. Like he wanted to and I did. So I just leaned in and kissed him."

"Whoa."

"Yeah."

"Except . . ." Gabby picks off a fluffy cloud of cotton candy and pops it in her mouth. "Once I was halfway up the ladder, I felt really weird. Like I'd made a big mistake. I wasn't even sure if I liked him. And I kind of wanted to go hide in my bedroom. Except I was at a pool party with the whole soccer team." She cringes. "So, that was awkward."

But still, I think. *You got to kiss Avery.*

"Anyway . . . I didn't realize how much you liked him. I mean, we never really talked a lot about stuff like that, you and me. It wasn't obvious from how you acted around him—I just thought you guys were friends."

"We are," I say. "I mean, I had this crush on him, but . . . I think I'm over it now."

269

Kiersten runs over to us, clutching her bag of cotton candy. "Well, that was a waste of money."

"I could've told you that," Gabby says.

"What'd she say?" I ask.

"She said I'm going to live to be one hundred and eleven years old and that I'll fall tragically in love with someone. But then she wouldn't say who!"

"Sounds like a fortune-teller." I catch Gabby's eye after she says it.

All three of us look around, trying to figure out where to go next.

"Want to go on the Ferris wheel?" Gabby asks.

It's straight ahead of us, looming over the whole fair. The sun is close to setting. We'd still have a pretty great view from the top.

"I don't know," Kiersten says. We watch as it turns ever so slowly.

"Hey!" calls a familiar voice from behind us.

"I heard you found your dog," Gregg says just as I'm turning around. "And your house is almost done, too, right?"

"Yup. Avery helped me find Hank. It was pretty awesome. We're living in a trailer for the beginning of the school year, but hopefully the house will be done before Thanksgiving."

"A trailer? Wow. That sounds fun. Like camping!"

"Sort of like camping. Except for a lot longer." There's something different about Gregg, and I can't totally figure it out. Did he get a new haircut? Is it his clothes? For the first time, he looks less like spontaneous-chicken Gregg and more like his brother.

"Well, I gotta go find my dad. Maybe I'll see you guys around later?"

"Yeah," I say. "Bye, Gregg."

As he walks away, I think about what Avery told me about Gregg. And the emails. Maybe when Gabby kept bringing up Gregg, she wasn't thinking about the Gregg who'd been our class clown since kindergarten. Maybe she saw something in Gregg that the rest of us couldn't see, the way you only can when you're the new girl.

"You know what's weird?" Kiersten says.

"Um, that gigantic banana with dreadlocks?" I point at the man in the white tank top passing by with a ginormous stuffed banana in his arms.

"No," Kiersten says. "Though that is also quite strange. Anyway! I was just thinking how there are all these people around us at the carnival. All these strangers, right? Well, maybe not. I mean, so they're strangers now. But in a few weeks, we'll be in school with them. Some of them will become our classmates. Our good friends. Our rivals. Our *boyfriends*. Okay, maybe not that. But maybe! Right?"

Gabriella nods.

I start looking at the faces in the crowd differently after she says it. Not the older people—the moms and dads and grandparents. And not the little kids either. But the ones that look our age. That boy with the pimply forehead and scuffed-up Vans. I could know him. Or that girl with the short, curly blond hair who's rolling her eyes at her mom. She might end up being my friend. A minute ago, they were just faces in the crowd to me. Perfect strangers. But now they're not. They're people with their own complicated lives, maybe more complicated than mine. And I could know them. Someday. Maybe someday soon.

And then my eyes latch onto a different kind of face. A familiar one. Brown hair sticking out of a dirty Red Sox hat. Navy-blue T-shirt. Khaki shorts. Thumbnails he needs to stop biting but probably won't.

"Avery!" He looks up when I say his name.

"I thought you were out of town already," Kiersten says as he approaches.

"It's not *that* far away," Avery says. "I mean, a different school, but I'll still come around. You're not rid of me yet!"

"We're trying to convince Kiersten to ride the Ferris wheel," Gabriella says.

"What, are you afraid of heights or something?" Avery challenges her.

"No!" Kiersten says. "It just looks really rickety. These things fall apart sometimes. People get hurt. I want to live to experience seventh grade, you know?"

"I think your odds of getting crushed to death by a

slowly dismantling Ferris wheel are pretty low," Avery says. "Like one in twenty-four million."

"You really know that?" I ask.

Avery nods. "I looked it up once."

"One in twenty-four million, huh?" Kiersten peers up toward the top of the Ferris wheel and sucks in a deep breath. "Okay, I'll do it. You in, Gabby?"

Gabriella nods.

All four of us get in line.

As they load up the people ahead of us, I notice that there are only two spots in each Ferris wheel car. I wonder who's going to sit with whom, but no one brings it up. We start talking about how excited we are for school to start and our class schedules and then suddenly we're at the front of the line.

"I need two of youse guys," the carnival worker says. "Let's make it snappy." He's got the beginnings of a mustache, and the tone of his voice tells me he isn't a huge fan of his job.

"I'll go," I say, stepping out. Kiersten starts to follow me.

"Wait," Avery jumps in behind me. "I kind of promised."

Kiersten and Gabriella look on from the sidelines, confused, and wait for the next car.

He remembers.

As I step in, the whole car shakes from side to side. I sit down on the metal seat. Avery sits across from me.

The carnival worker closes the little metal door on the side—the only thing holding us in—and I suck in a breath. Kiersten's right about one thing. This ride *is* pretty rickety.

And with a jolt—we're off.

I close my eyes. I didn't think I was afraid of heights, but maybe I am, because I don't want to look down. Or up. Or at Avery. I keep them closed.

"You too, huh?"

"It didn't look this scary from the ground." There's no bar for your hands like on other rides. I clasp mine together. I wonder how many times we're going to go around. How long until we're off this thing.

"Oh, wow!" Avery says.

"What?"

"I'm not going to tell you. You need to open your eyes to find out."

"That's not fair."

But Avery doesn't give in.

I take in a deep breath, listen to my heart slow down a little, and open my eyes. "Oh my goodness. Whoa."

We're stopped halfway up while some new riders get on down below. I can see the whole town, or at least most of it, from here. "There's the library and the grocery store and the stoplight and the church. And our hill. Our street." Hollow Road. I can see how the tornado cut right across our town. Divided it in two.

It was wide; the news said it was almost a mile wide at points. A whole mile. I can barely run the mile in gym. Four times around the track. The tornado was *that* wide.

But the crazy thing is how, from up here, everything looks so small. My town, where I've lived my whole life—it's *tiny*. There's this whole big world out there, stretching far off into the horizon. Starting junior high? That's only the first step.

"Pretty cool, huh?" Avery says.

"Yeah."

We start moving again. We reach the top, not even stopping there, and go lower, lower, lower, past the carnival worker, and then up again. I'm not sure how this works. How many times we get to go around and around before we have to get off for good. All I know is I want to stay right here, in this Ferris wheel car with Avery. Just like this.

"I can't believe you're not going to be at our school."

"I'm only fifteen minutes away," he says. "I timed it and everything."

"Only fifteen? Really?"

"Yeah," he says. "You know, I spent the whole summer being worried about moving and leaving everyone. I couldn't enjoy hanging out with my friends because it felt like it was all going to end. It seemed easier to just . . . be by myself sometimes."

I think about how often I found him at the McLarens' playing computer games on his laptop with his headphones on. Totally in the zone, I thought. More like totally alone.

"But now that just feels so stupid. Moving isn't the worst thing in the world. I'm still close by. I'll still be able to go over to my friends' houses. And you guys can come out to Palmer anytime." He looks directly at me when he says it.

Avery takes in a deep breath and lets it out, and suddenly I'm back in the car with him, on that ride home that brought us to houses that weren't even there anymore. Just me and Avery in the backseat. Avery holding my hand and reminding me to breathe. I can almost hear the sirens and the chain saws again. Almost.

He clears his throat. "You know, when I get mad or frustrated about everything that happened, I try to remember that the tornado didn't get me. It just got my house. I'm still here."

Our car is lowering again, and I can feel it in my heart: I know we're the next ones that'll have to get off. The people walking the fairgrounds are growing larger and larger. We're getting closer and closer to the ground. We're quiet, me and Avery, and I wonder what he's thinking right now. My friend Avery, right across from me.

I know what I'm thinking.

We're still here.

Acknowledgments

Growing up in Massachusetts, you never think you're going to encounter a tornado. A hurricane, sure. Blizzards: been there, done that. But an EF-3 tornado? Definitely not. And yet on a June evening in 2011, an EF3 tornado crossed the street where I grew up, wreaking devastation on my tiny hometown, Sturbridge, and neighboring communities. While my parents' home, half a mile away from the tornado's path, was spared, many others were not so fortunate, and their stories reported in the local newspapers and TV news will stick with me for a long time. Though *14 Hollow Road* is a work of fiction, this particular tornado informed my understanding of how a tornado could impact a small rural town like the invented Hitchcock. I also must credit one of the most fantastic and enduring episodes of *This American Life,* "186: Prom," which focuses on the true story of an early-summer night in 2001 in which a tornado destroyed a third of Hoisington, Kansas, while high school seniors danced the night away. It is one of my all-time favorite episodes and made me wonder how a similar event could shape a girl on the cusp of becoming a teenager. If you haven't listened to it yet, I highly recommend tuning in.

The journey from a speck of an idea to an actual story is long and winding. This novel grew out of a workshop piece at Vermont College of Fine Arts, and I'm grateful to the participants, whose thoughtful feedback helped develop the work in progress, particularly workshop leaders A. S. King and Alan Cumyn. As always, I'm deeply appreciative of Katie Grimm's many careful reads and boundless enthusiasm. Kelly Delaney, you saw and articulated the heart of this book better than I could at that stage; revising with you has been such a joy. The entire team at Knopf has been a delight to work with. Special thanks to illustrator extraordinaire Erin McGuire for a stunning cover image that perfectly captures the swirl of emotions spun up by the storm.

I feel fortunate to have found the writing communities who made the sophomore book endeavor way less scary than I expected it to be. My Magic Sevens, who willingly read draft after draft, offering advice at key moments, Robin Kirk, Ellen Reagan, Cynthia Surrisi, Anne Bowen, Kelly Dyksterhouse, and Stephanie Farrow: thank you for your friendship and your wisdom. Autumn Krause, my cheerleader, and all of the M.A.G.I.C. I.F.s: thank you for being there every step of the way. The Sweet Sixteens had to be the most ideal companions on the debut journey that I could have ever imagined. The Middle Grade Writers'

Guild has been such a touchstone for me through all the ups and downs of the past two years (and approximately five billion questions about publishing). Love you, girls! Though I've left the Boston area—sniffles—the YA writers' crepe meet-up in Somerville is never far from my heart. Thank you for welcoming me into your circle, despite the fact that I never once ate a crepe and I write middle-grade.

I have to give an extended shout-out to those who do the magical work of connecting books with young readers. No author would be anywhere without their countless hours on the front lines. I'd like to thank the Nerdy Book Club, especially Colby Sharp, and all the teachers and librarians I met during the publication journey for *The Distance to Home*. I will never forget your support of my debut. Your enthusiasm and the stories you've shared with me of young readers who responded to my writing mean more than I can ever say. Ted Schelvan, Shauna Yusko, Patti Tjomsland, Mike Fleming, Alissa Lauzon, and Janet Hilbun, thank you for your continued support. BFYA forever!

To my parents, Robert and Lynn Barnes—without whom I would not exist, never mind be a writer—thank you for handing out bookmarks to anyone with a pulse. In all seriousness, thank you for everything. To my husband, Colin, for your continued support of my dream. To my friends and family, for listening and learning more about children's literature than you ever needed to know. To my cat, Lilly, for keeping my ego in check with scratches and hisses. Thank you, thank you always. And for Kai Barnes, because it is very cool to see your name in the acknowledgments of a published book when you are in elementary school.

But most of all, thank you, the reader.

About the Author

Jenn Bishop is also the author of *The Distance to Home* and is a former youth services and teen librarian. She is a graduate of the University of Chicago, where she studied English, and the Vermont College of Fine Arts, where she received her MFA in Writing for Children and Young Adults. Along with her husband and cat, Jenn lives in Cincinnati. Visit her online at JennBishop.com or on Twitter at @buffalojenn.